Katrina

AARON BOWLES

Lisa Nicole Publishing
Lisanicolealexander.com
Gotha, FL 34734

Printed in the United States of America

ISBN: 978-1-7356342-8-9

Dear Katrina,

This is Dr. Oni. I am reaching out to you because I was concerned about how things went with my assistance in your situation a while ago. First, let me tell you that I am sorry. I have done some much-needed soul searching. You and your friend Tiffany came to my office in Kenya, wanting me to lift the curse I placed over your love life. After watching you walk out of my office as a broken woman, I felt sorry for the mess I had made. I felt as if I was partly responsible for your problem. The way I have always dealt with my practices in the past was to never talk to anyone that I placed that curse on because of what may or may not happen. I understood that people always wanted more than they had, even though their current situation was perfect. Know that nothing is 100% perfect. Everyone loves the idea of having that special someone in their life that makes them happy and treats them well.

Bringing this to people's attention was all I wanted. It was never meant to destroy lives but to open ones' mind to understand what true appreciation is. I do not believe that each person has only one soulmate.

Maybe after destroying their first relationship, I could only hope that they would leave well enough alone and just be happy with the next relationship they get into. So, I am writing this letter to you because after researching and following some of the people I helped in the past, I found out only 1/3 of my patients got the understanding, 1/3 suffered from heavy depression, and 1/3 committed suicide. I do not know your current situation, but if by any chance you still want me to lift the curse, I will. I am truly sorry for my interference in your marriage. I should have just suggested a therapist and counseling.

Sincerely,

Dr. Oni

CHAPTER ONE

Puppy Love

On May 6th 2015, Katrina was sitting on a bench at the airport holding a letter from Dr. Oni. The letter was open as tears flowed down her face, along with the weather to match her spirits. The letter brought back so many memories. She started reminiscing about the life she once had and how it all started.

* * *

When Katrina was little, she was a daddy's girl. She loved him so much that she patterned her prince charming after him. Her father was a hardworking, kind-hearted, loving, very spiritual, and charming man. Katrina's father's name was Joseph Moore. People knew him as Mr. Joe, and he was well respected in the neighborhood. He owned a mechanic shop that he had built from the ground up. He never let work get in the way of his family. He was a true example of being a man, and the way her mother loved him was only seen in fairytales.

Their marriage was admired and envied because it seemed that it was the essence of true love. Growing up, it was Katrina's dream to find a man like that. Her high school sweetheart was the spitting image of her father. His name was Trey Valentine. He was a superstar athlete and a stellar student. Growing up, all the girls wanted him, but he only had eyes for Katrina. They started dating in 8th grade, and she knew then that Trey would be hers forever. They would often talk about getting married, going on an expensive honeymoon, all the kids they would have, their future careers, and the places they wanted to live.

Trey and Katrina even applied to the same colleges. A few of those colleges offered both Katrina and Trey academic scholarships. Trey had multiple scholarship offers in sports as well. They had it all mapped out, but sometimes plans don't go the way we want. Trey's dream was to become a lawyer, and he received an academic scholarship to attend one of the most prestigious law schools in the country. He knew that this would break Katrina's heart and was willing and even planning to turn the opportunity down to be with Katrina.

His parents weren't having it. Katrina and Trey's parents had a sit-down with them and shared their advice about relationships and life. They had very solid input and old sayings such as "if you love someone, you should set them free, and if they are meant to be yours, they will come back to you." So if they loved each other, they would do what was best for each other, and that distance shouldn't break them up.

* * *

Katrina can still remember the conversation they had the day they broke up. It was 2008, their freshman year of college. They were both attending different schools but still making their relationship work. Both she and Trey were taking finals, and distance was really becoming a hassle. Neither one was willing to sacrifice failing school to go to see the other. It also cost money and plenty of drive time to keep their relationship going. Trey tried to convince her things would change after finals. He felt that it was his fault they were in different locations, so he pleaded and begged her to change her mind. Katrina was very firm on calling it quits and felt it was time to explore her options. She was a very beautiful woman, and guys would constantly try to talk to her, but she was always very loyal to Trey.

It bothered her that she grew up having her lover close throughout high school. Now that they were in college, they could not see each other like they used to. It was not like she needed a man to maintain her, but she *did* want consistent companionship. So she went through a few options, but no young man caught her eye.

Tiffany, her best friend since childhood, went to the same college as she did. She was one of those friends that were not the type to settle down. Tiffany was only a year older than Katrina, yet it seemed like she had *five* years more experience. Tiffany always had stories to tell of her sex life and how she made men spend their money and time with her. They did everything together. Tiffany was like the big sister she never had.

CHAPTER TWO

Frat Boy Dallas

One day Tiffany asked Katrina to go to a frat party with her. Katrina was going through a tough time because of the breakup with Trey, and she had finals all in the same week. She was reluctant to go, let alone have a good time and meet new people. But as usual, Tiffany could always talk her into doing things she didn't want to do. Later that night, they went to a frat party, and things got a little wild. There was lots of drinking and loud music blasting. Being the friend she is, Tiffany was trying to get Katrina to forget all about her problems and gave her *way* too many drinks.

Tiffany got a little distracted with a few of the guys she had previous encounters with at the party. She was moving around all night, trying to avoid these guys and not get caught up. So for a few hours, Katrina was left by herself. Some guys who had too many drinks started plotting on who would be the first to break in some freshman booty. They noticed Katrina sitting alone, leaning in her chair. So a few fellas approached her, trying to spit game. One managed to talk Katrina into going to a quieter place to talk.

As they began to go, Katrina could barely walk on her own and leaned up against the guy for support. He placed her arm around his neck and proceeded to walk upstairs. Tiffany noticed the guy walking with Katrina but didn't pay much attention to it. That was until she saw them going upstairs. A group of guys followed them, with crazy looks on their faces as if they had the intent to take turns on her. Tiffany saw a friend of hers that was at the party and quickly ran over to him. She pointed upstairs and pleaded for him to go stop whatever was about to happen.

The guy that was with Katrina got her to a room and laid her down. He talked to her as if he was a good guy, telling her she should just lay down and take a nap. Then, in walked a group of guys as Katrina was laid out, not knowing what was about to happen to her. While the group of guys began to undress next to the incapacitated Katrina, the door opened, and a few more guys walked in. This group of guys was not there to have their turns. They wanted to know what the hell was going on!

Tiffany's friend Dallas was asking the majority of questions. Being one of the fraternity brothers and a resident of that frat house, he saw things going very wrong in this situation.

Dallas went through the group of guys, cursing them out as he helped Katrina put her clothes back on. The group of guys who were about to rape her took offense to how Dallas tried scolding them and wanted to fight. But the other brothers that came with Dallas were ready to kick ass on whoever wanted it. Dallas grabbed Katrina and got what little information he could get out of her. She told him that she came to the party with her friend Tiffany and didn't know where she was. Dallas, already knowing who Tiffany was, sent one of his brothers down to get her so they could escort them home.

* * *

The next day Katrina woke up with the worst headache, and Tiffany was lying beside her just as sick. Katrina stumbled to get up, and as she was making her way to the bathroom, she heard people in the living room arguing. She woke Tiffany up and asked her who the hell was in the house with them.

"Girl, that's just Dallas with his fine ass. He walked us home and made sure nobody did anything to us. I guess he fell asleep on the couch," Tiffany told her.

"I don't know who the girl is, probably one of his little whores bitching at him for being here. She probably thinks he's screwing somebody in here. He thinks he's a playa, but he's good people though. Go out there and see what's going on."

"Naw imma wait. And how in the hell did I walk that far? I don't remember *anything* about last night. All I know is that I am done drinking and letting your butt talk me into stuff. But for right now, his butt needs to get out of my apartment with that mess. I don't need these hoes around here trying to beat me up all over a misunderstanding. Since you know him, then you need to tell him to go somewhere else with that stuff," Katrina replied.

"That's right girl," Tiffany said, "imma tell Dallas...who was the one that *saved* your ass from being raped last night to leave before your ungrateful ass thanks him?! DOUBT IT!"

"WTF do you mean from being raped? Did I pass out at that party? Please tell me that I wasn't that stupid!" Katrina said as she ran to the bathroom to check herself.

Panicking, Katrina yelled,

"No No No" as if somebody did something to her.

She checked out just fine as she stepped out of the bathroom feeling like an ass for wanting to kick him out of her place. She sat down and waited for things to quiet down before she walked into the living room to meet Dallas and thank him.

She walked into the living room to introduce herself, and the other girl becomes irate and started yelling! Dallas quickly told her he was done with her insecure ass, and she needed to leave and never call him again. He put her out, slammed the door in the young lady's face, and turned around to see Katrina in the same outfit she wore last night. He commented on how he thought she might need to shower because she smelled like alcohol. They both laughed and looked at each other in a joking manner.

"I'm so sorry that I caused you any trouble. It wasn't my intention to even be at your party, but my friend Tiffany made me come," she told Dallas.

"It's all good. I never wanted her anyway, it was just sex, and she wanted more than that. So really, I should be thanking you for giving me a good reason to tell her to kick rocks. She was *way* too clingy and obsessive," Dallas replied.

"Well... anyway (as she rolled her eyes), thank you for keeping my life out of danger and keeping me out of therapy because Lord knows I would have needed it. You don't know how much that means to me. If I told my father what you did for me, two or three things would happen," she replied.

"Like what, I'm the good guy here?

"Naw, I'm saying he would be in your debt forever for being there for me! He would probably adopt you as the son he never had and definitely would have killed those jackasses who tried to rape me." Katrina replied.

"Well, let's not tell him then because we don't need anybody getting killed. They need their asses beat, but karma is a bitch, you know. Plus, I don't need your dad constantly calling me asking me what you are doing, as if I'm constantly watching over you. I mean, I see you around and notice you, but I'm not watching your ass," he laughed. "And if he wants me to be his son, his daughter needs to let me take her out first."

"How dare you try and capitalize just because you saved me," Katrina replied jokingly.

"I'm not trying to get beat up by all the girls you talked to. Lord only knows how many that is, and I'm just a freshman. I've got four or maybe five years until I graduate. I don't want to fight every week."

"Girl, please, ain't nothing going to happen to you, I promise. Don't make me call your daddy myself. I'm pretty sure he would give me your number now anyway, after what I did for you. I'm the good guy, remember? Hell, he owes *me* now!" Dallas replied.

They both laughed really hard.

"I don't know," Katrina said. "I don't need any more trouble in my life. Plus, I got finals, and I need to study."

"We ALL got finals, but I understand. That's cool. Well, if you see me on campus, don't be a stranger, you dig?" said Dallas.

Tiffany yelled from the bedroom, "Bitch, you know you want to go. Stop playing hard to get and go. Hell, he did save that pussy!"

Katrina smiled and said to Dallas, "I'll tell you what, we can go out, but you better not treat me like them other hoes. Better yet, just get rid of them because I'm not going for the drama. Do you know what chivalry is? I want all that and then some."

"That's a bet, and yes, I know what chivalry is. Let's do something this weekend. You pick the spot," Dallas replied.

That weekend they met up and went out. Things flowed smoothly, and they clicked really well. As time went on, Katrina and Dallas became the young power couple on campus. Katrina pledged to a sorority and her status made a come up on campus. She became who the girls wanted to be like, and the men wanted to be with. Throughout their college years, she and Dallas had a great relationship. There were a few incidents when women would always find a way to bring Dallas's name up in cheating situations, but Dallas and Katrina stayed strong with their love.

* * *

On the day of Dallas's graduation, things were going well as usual. Katrina hung out with Dallas and his family all day. It was a perfect day for Katrina. She saw a man that had things going for himself, and the love he showed her daily was wonderful. This was the life she had imagined. When they got to the graduation, they kissed each other and parted ways so that he could take his seat with the other graduates.

When Dallas's name was called, he stood up and walked towards the stage. The crowd clapped for all graduates when they were called to walk across the stage and receive their degrees. But the cheering in the crowd seemed a little unusual when Dallas started walking. Katrina and his family looked strangely at one another and tried to see who was doing all that cheering. Shouting a few rows back was a beautiful woman with a child. The child she was holding shouted, "yeah, daddy!" Katrina looked at the family very cluelessly, but their faces could not hide the truth. She could see that they knew who the woman was.

Katrina jumped up and ran out, which grabbed everyone's attention. Dallas looked into the crowd and saw Katrina exiting as she pardoned herself through the crowd. He looked in the crowd to see who was still congratulating him and saw who it was. The look on his face told it all. Even the crowd knew what was going on just by his expression. In disbelief, Katrina sat in the passenger seat of his car and waited on him until after the graduation ceremony. As he was coming out of the building, he noticed that Katrina was still waiting on him.

Dallas didn't know for sure if Katrina saw him or not, but he got in the car with his family, trying to avoid her at all costs. He never showed up, nor did he call to explain. That day changed Katrina. From that day on, she became a bitter person.

CHAPTER THREE

Trey is Back

Senior year came pretty quickly as Katrina distanced herself from the world and dedicated her time to her studies. After she graduated, she was given a job as an accountant at a bank back home by a family friend. As much as she didn't want to go home, it was the best startup job for her career and ideal for her to be around family. She had been home for 18 months and was in the market to buy her first home. She had been looking at some nice homes not too far from her family and within walking distance to her office. She attended a few open houses, but most of the houses were priced too high and out of her budget.

On her way home from work one day, she decided to park her car and take a stroll through the neighborhood of some homes that had caught her eye. While walking up to a house she had previously visited, Katrina noticed a man posting real estate agent signs in front yards. To her surprise she recognized him. It was her high school sweetheart Trey!

Katrina was so shocked to see him that she kept walking past the home and eventually turned around to head back to her car. Later that night, she drove back to the area and wrote down his phone number from one of the signs, only to realize that his number had never changed. Katrina gave him a call just out of curiosity to see how he had been. She also wanted to see if he could talk to the family of the home that she was interested in. She wanted them to bring down their price so she could buy it. Trey was so excited to hear from her that he nearly forgot about the home and mainly wanted to focus more on catching up and taking her out on a date. She told him yes, but only if he promised to help her get the home, in a joking manner. Her answer may have seemed very selfish, but he agreed to it. He didn't pay much attention to the fact that it seemed that she would only go out with him if he did something for her.

Trey kept his promise to help Katrina get the house but could not talk the owners down far enough. So, he cut his percentage of the profit off of the price. Still a little bit over her budget, and with Trey making no profit on it himself, Katrina accepted the deal. Trey was happy for her, but honestly, he just wanted the chance to win her heart again.

With their history, you would think it wouldn't take much to rekindle that fire. But Dallas had really messed up her trust, and it bled into their conversations constantly. Trey would always have to plead his case and remind her that he is not Dallas and that *she* was the one who broke up with *him*. Even though distance was not an issue anymore, she still had her reservations. Katrina gave Trey a hard time trying to get back into her life. It took a few months of being persistent and understanding of her feelings about trust.

Meanwhile, Trey was growing a little weary because his feelings had never changed, but hers had. He was constantly reminding her of how he would treat her right and that his track record proved that a long time ago. Katrina broke down and started to remember how hard he tried. She remembered how much her family liked him and that it's not like starting all over with a man she doesn't know. They started dating again, and it took no time for her to realize she had almost lost out on having this man in her life again. They dated for two months and made it official that they were now officially in a relationship.

CHAPTER FOUR
The Move-In

One month later, Katrina wanted to shake things up a bit. She asked Trey to come over because she needed his assistance. As he pulled up, she was standing at the front door. He got out of the car and asked her what was going on. She walked to the passenger side of his car, opened the door, and told him to get in.

"I'm taking you out, and it's on me, boo!"

He walked towards her with this odd look on his face, smiled, and got in. After they came back from dinner, she pulled into the driveway, parked the car, and ran to Trey's side of the vehicle to open his door. He shook his head and stepped out of the car, telling her she was acting like a true gentleman in a joking tone.

They walked up to the house, and when she opened the door, all he could see were rose petals on the floor leading up to the bedroom. She made him wait to go upstairs as she lit candles and poured him a glass of wine. Then she ran upstairs to the bathroom to run his bathwater.

"Baby, what's going on? You asked me to come over here to help you, but I haven't helped you with anything!"

Katrina came down and asked Trey to get naked. Almost spitting his wine out in shock, he complied. The bathwater was ready as he entered the room, and she poured him another glass of wine. As the night was coming to an end, Katrina wanted to talk to Trey.

"Well, Trey, we have been rocking with each other for a few months, and it didn't take long for me to love you again. My feelings for you have never changed. You are still the man I loved in high school, and you are just as fine as you were back then," Katrina shared.

"Baby, you have done all these things for me today. It's not my birthday, and I *know* it's not our anniversary. What you got up your sleeves? Don't tell me that you're pregnant!" Trey replied.

"Boy naw, I'm not pregnant!" Katrina exclaimed.

"Well, are you proposing?" Trey asked.

"Naw boy, that's your job!" Katrina replied.

Trey jumped out of the tub without drying off and got down on one knee.

"Katrina, I have loved you from the first time I saw you and still do to this very day. Baby, I have never stopped loving you. I don't have a ring right now, but that doesn't mean I don't want to marry you. Just give me a little time, and I will put that rock on your hand."

Katrina smiled. "I know this, and it doesn't have to take that long. Heck, I don't even need a ring until you pass your boards. And actually, you can move in with me so that you can save on your bills, and we can make this work baby!"

"Dang baby, that's like music to my ears, but I'm the man. I'll pay the bills, and you cover me for everything else. How soon were you thinking?" Trey asked.

"I'm talking in the next few weeks!" replied Katrina.

"Say no more baby; it's already done! Baby, do you remember what our parents said before we went off to college? If it was meant to be, things would work themselves out, and we would be together again. Look at GOD!!!" Trey exclaimed as they both smiled and laughed.

CHAPTER FIVE

In the Airport

Snapping back from her memories, she is still sitting on the bench, looking out the window. Out of nowhere, an old lady walks up beside her and offers her a shoulder to cry on and an ear to listen. The older woman states that she was walking by and saw Katrina's face full of sorrow and that she looked as if she needed someone to be there for her.

"Honey," she said, "I know you don't know me, but I refuse to let a beautiful, yet sad soul sit in this airport on a rainy day as if she just did something so unforgivable. Sweet baby, what's going on?"

"I'm sorry, ma'am for looking so distraught and like I need somebody to be here for me. I'm sure you know a lot, but my situation sounds so dumb and unreal I'm ashamed to tell anybody about it." Katrina replied.

The old lady said, "Child, listen to me and listen well. Do you believe in GOD?"

Katrina nods her head yes.

"So how do you know GOD did not send me back home this way? I never take this route home, sweetheart. My son normally sends me home on a train. For some reason, I just felt like flying home on the rainiest of days. Go figure."

"Ok," Katrina said, "I'll take you up on that offer to talk. I'll just tell you the meat of it because I don't want to talk your ear off. It's all about how I screwed up my marriage *and* other people's lives."

The old lady looked at Katrina and said, "There is nothing that you can't be forgiven for. Take your time. I have nothing to do when I get home but feed my birds and watch television. The truth is I hardly ever talk to people anymore. Just to sit here, be in your company, and listen to your story will make my week."

So, Katrina starts telling her side of the story from the day her friends put the thought of her husband cheating on her into her head.

CHAPTER SIX

Girls Night

Years passed by, and the love that Katrina and Trey shared was beautiful. They had gotten married, and life was exactly how she imagined it would be. One day, her friend Tiffany called because she would be in town for a week and wanted to catch up with her homie. Tiffany was still as wild as she was in college but had a boyfriend this time, *with* the potential to marry. Katrina knew Tiffany actually came to town to visit some old flames. Tiffany suggested they have a night out and call up some old high school girls they used to know and go clubbing and grab a few drinks. Katrina reminded her of the last time they went drinking what happened.

"Girl, I'm not going drinking with your ass. The last time I did that, I was almost raped!" Katrina told Tiffany.

"Heffa, nobody is trying to drink like that. I just want to go out and kick it with my bitches. It's been far too long and way past due. So you better show up, or we gon fight. You know you my day one. Plus, you married to Trey fine ass, and y'all got it made!" Tiffany replied.

"And you know this! Alright, girl I'll come out. I've needed to get out of the house anyway. Me and Trey stay in each other's faces 24/7 365," Katrina replied as she gave in.

Later that night, Katrina and Tiffany linked up with a few friends, and they were all having a good time. They started sharing stories of their lives and how things were going. As usual, when alcohol is present, feelings rise. The girls started spilling their hearts out about their relationships and comparing themselves to one another. Compared to their situations, Katrina really *did* have the best life. She listened to her friends talk about how they started their relationships and the good times they had! Then they started sharing the bad things that were going on in their relationships. They shared how their boyfriends and husbands cheated on them. They thought it was so funny how the husbands thought they were getting away with it, but *they* were having affairs too!

Katrina sat back, thanking GOD for the man she was blessed with. She recalled the time she was cheated on by Dallas and the child he had due to his infidelity. She was so blinded by love that she ignored all the signs until it was too late. Katrina blurted out while still thinking about Dallas and the way he did her.

"Can you believe he even had the audacity to text me how sorry he was? Hell, he wasn't even man enough to *call* me!"

Tiffany said, "Wait, who just text you?"

"Nobody," Katrina said. "I was just thinking of how Dallas did me."

"Well, what did he do?" Tiffany asked.

Katrina told her everything, and she was shocked!

"Why am I just finding out the truth on why y'all broke up? I saw him a few months ago and chit-chatted with him. I even went down memory lane with him on how I thought y'all would make it. He was like she deserved better, and it was just time we broke up. He never went into details, and now I know why. Dirty dog!!" Tiffany replied.

"Girl, I found out on his graduation as he walked across the stage," Katrina said. "I saw that bitch there cheering him on with their daughter. I just got up and left and didn't even look back because I knew he saw me leaving."

"Girl, I would have snatched that bitch up for you!" Tiffany said.

"And that's exactly why I didn't tell you. The worst part of it was I waited in his car, and he didn't even come back. Left my ass there looking foolish." Katrina shared.

"Well, you are way better than me. But look at you now, back with your high school sweetheart and shit. Y'all were meant to be anyways. I'm happy for you," Tiffany replied.

"Well, when will I get the chance to meet the man who slayed you?" Katrina asked Tiffany.

"In due time. I got to see how much of my shit he can take before I take him seriously."

Katrina shook her head and took another drink.

CHAPTER SEVEN

Signs

As she moved on in her story while talking to the older lady, she picked up at the point when she first noticed a few signs. The first day she noticed, it was about 10 o'clock at night. Trey had just finished cooking a late dinner for them, and they were having a movie night. His phone rang, and an unfamiliar number popped up. Katrina looked at it, but Trey quickly put it on silent and flipped the phone over. This brought suspicion to Katrina's mind, but she never made a fuss about it. Then the phone rang again. Trey looked at the phone, saw what number it was, muted it again, and placed the phone back on its face. Before he could do it again, Katrina quickly tried to remember the number the best she could. She believed she had caught enough of the number to figure it out.

Just one or two numbers off, she tried calling the number back the next day while she was at work. Neither number she called was right. So now she was thrown for a loop. She didn't want to ask him because it would seem as if she didn't trust him.

The last thing she wanted to do was start a problem with a great man. Weeks went by, and the number called again. Being that it was close to midnight, this pissed her off. As much as she wanted to answer the phone, it was not her place to be answering Trey's phone. Trey walked out of the bathroom from the shower, jumped right into bed, and engaged in sex with Katrina. As much as this was playing in her mind, she did not want to mess up their night or go to bed mad, so she left it alone. Katrina replayed the number over and over in her head as she went to sleep. The plan was to remember it and call it in the morning.

She woke up early the next day with a sense of urgency in her walk. Katrina could hardly *wait* to get to work so that she could call. Once making it to work, she shut the door to her office. She called the number numerous times but was not getting an answer. The phone recorder kept playing back, "the google subscriber that you are calling cannot be reached at this time." Katrina was confused, thinking that she still didn't call the right number. With a puzzled look on her face, she started going over all the things her friends said about their significant others and how they cheated.

The unexpected phone calls were one of the most commonly talked about signs of cheating. She immediately called Tiffany and told her that she thinks Trey was cheating. For the first time that Katrina could remember, Tiffany had the level head. She told Katrina she was just imagining things and it could be nothing. But if she wanted her to, she could help her find out. They devised a plan to catch Trey. They began to watch his every move, yet it seemed as if his days were as normal as they always were. They both figured that maybe he was just one of the few guys who actually knew *how* to cheat.

CHAPTER EIGHT

Desperation

Getting desperate to find out if Trey was cheating and covering his tracks well, Katrina hired a private investigator. The private investigator followed Trey for about three weeks and reported back to Katrina. He told her that he could not find anything abnormal, and that Trey seemed like a stand-up guy. So, Katrina decided to leave it alone. That is until she was bothered by that number again during another late night with Trey. Only this time she asked him to answer the phone, and he said no. This quickly seemed to be a red flag to her.

"Trey, you need to answer your phone. This is not the first time I have seen that number call you. I even tried to call it back, and they won't answer for me. Who is she, and why is she calling so late?" Katrina exclaimed.

"You tripping," Trey said. "Ain't nobody cheating on you. That's business, and I don't feel like answering the phone."

"I told Wes about calling my phone so late at night, and he continues to do it. This is my way of teaching him a lesson."

"Really, Trey?" Katrina replied.

"Yes," he said, "Really. Now drop it." Trey chimed back.

"Ok imma drop it, but you better keep your hoes in check," she said.

Time flew by, and that number was no longer a nuisance at night. But now, in the mornings, it was. It really bothered Katrina that Trey would not answer the phone in front of her. Now she was *convinced* it was a woman. She was desperate to find out because she would *never* let another man pull the wool over her eyes again.

So, she started searching online and googling how to catch your man cheating. She no longer wanted to hire the same private eye. She wanted *real* results. She went through at least 15 pages of PI's. Hiring people and purchasing number identifiers were just a waste of time. Just as she was about to give up, she saw a witch doctor located in Louisiana listed as a private eye, and it made her curious. In a joking manner, she wondered if he practiced black magic or voodoo being that he was from way down south.

She took the contact information down and decided to think about it. Shortly after writing it down, she decided to call the number.

"Hello, this is Dr. Oni. How may I be of service to you?"

"Are you really a doctor?" Katrina asked.

"Yes I am, and who do I have the pleasure of speaking with?"

"Oh, I'm so sorry, my name is Katrina, and I was looking for a private eye and came across your name six pages later. Why are you so far down on the list of agencies? Do you not produce results?"

"Well, this is more of a hobby than a career." Dr. Oni replied

"I have a 99.9% chance of helping you get the results you seek. Why are you asking me so many questions?"

"I only ask because I'm trying to build up the courage to ask for your help about something I might be overthinking," Katrina responded.

"Overthinking what?" Dr. Oni replied.

"Well, my husband has been nothing but good to me. But this strange number kept calling him, and he refused to pick it up in front of me. I have tried to call the number back, and whoever it is will not answer the phone. It's a google number, and I recently bought the number identifier app, but there is no name attached to it."

"I see why you would be concerned," said Dr. Oni. "Have you tried to talk to your husband about it and let him know your concerns?"

"Yes, I have, and he told me not to worry about it. That he was not cheating and that I should just let it go. I'm not satisfied with that answer, but I refuse to start problems in my home without hard evidence."

"So, my main question is, do you believe him, and how sure are you that he is having an affair?" Dr. Oni asked her.

"I don't know what to believe anymore! I was hurt once by a man who had a baby on me. I saw the warning signs but refused to believe my own eyes. Now, my gut tells me that Trey is not cheating on me, but my gut said that last time, and it was totally wrong."

"I have a crazy question for you. Your google search said witch doctor. I know you may be African with the name and all but are you really into witchcraft/ black magic?" Katrina asked.

"Some of my methods may use a little magic and a lot of luck, and it seems to work for me," he said.

"I only take on serious customers because I do not refund or undo what is done once I start.

"So I will give you a few days to think about it. Please call me back when you are ready and sure, ok?"

"Yes, Dr.," Katrina replied. "I need a few days to think about it. Thank you for your time. Talk to you later, sir."

CHAPTER NINE

It's Done

A few days passed by, and Katrina decided to call the doctor.

"Hello, you have reached Dr. Oni. How may I be of service?"

"Dr. Oni, It's Katrina. I called you a few days ago and told you I needed some time to think about if I wanted to go through with your expertise on catching my husband."

"Ah Katrina, I was just thinking of you and was expecting your call. So tell me, what is it that you think you want to find out, and what will you do after you get your answer?" Dr. Oni asked.

"Well, Doc, I have been heartbroken before, and I'm over people hiding things from me. When I find out for sure he is cheating, I will feel better knowing that no one else was able to pull the wool over my eyes and keep me in the dark. As far as leaving him, I still don't know because I am living my best life. If he is cheating, I'll figure out something when I get to that bridge."

"You said other people hid things from you, and what happened with that situation?" Dr. Oni asked.

"Dr. Oni, I'd rather not discuss it in detail but, my college lover/ex had me blinded by love only to blindside me with a baby at his graduation. I was in a dark place for a while after that. I'm over it now and just want to be on top of my game from now on. Taking heed to every red flag that comes up, you understand?"

"I do understand," said Dr. Oni, "just know my practice has a price, and things could go your way, or it could not go as planned."

"So you're telling me that I will not get any answers?" Katrina asked.

"No, I'm not saying that. You will get answers for sure, but it might not---"

"Doc, just do what you got to do. How much and when do we start?" Katrina cut him off.

"It starts now. Close your eyes. What I'm about to do is speak some words into your life. You will not know the meaning of these words, nor would you recognize them because they are of my native tongue and with a few spell words intertwined." (Dr. Oni starts speaking to her in a weird tongue and accent).

"Katrina, I want you to open your eyes and simply say SHOW ME."

Katrina repeated, "SHOW ME."

"So what I've done is curse your true love. What will happen now is that every time he has sex, the woman he is having sex with will not feel the pleasure of intercourse, but *you* will. From touching to kissing and penetration, you will feel it all."

"What kind of practice is that?" Katrina asks. "You mean to tell me that you just put a sex curse on folks, and it works? Why do I have to wait until he has sex with someone to find out? I thought you were going to make him reveal to me that he was cheating or something of that nature."

"Katrina, you called me and wanted my help. I told you that my spell would get you results. You explained to me that you and your friends and other private eyes could not catch him, right?" Dr. Oni replied.

"Yes, that's correct, "Katrina said.

"Well, give my practice a chance. And if you don't receive an answer sooner than a few months, you don't have to pay me. Just know that the things you are searching for will come to light, and I pray you handle it as gently as possible, and no one gets hurt."

"Dr. Oni, I meant no harm. I'm just anxious about finding out. Thank you and will try my best to handle the issue like a real woman." Katrina replied.

Katrina got off the phone and immediately called Tiffany. They discussed what she and Dr. Oni talked about and how she didn't have to pay anything. She was so amped up about catching Trey cheating on her that it was almost an obsession.

"Girl, you over there practicing black magic and shit. What's wrong with you?" Tiffany said. "Are you that hyped about catching Trey?"

"Let us not forget how Dallas did me. Damn near four years of my life with that man, and he had a whole damn baby on me. I was a fool then, but not now." Katrina said.

"Trey and Dallas are two different dudes," Tiffany told her. "But I feel you. I just hate you went this far to find out. You are going to hell, voodoo lady," as she laughed.

CHAPTER TEN

The First Feeling

Soon they talked about linking up again with the girls and having another ladies' night out, claiming it was well needed. As the days passed by since talking to Dr. Oni, nothing happened. The days were just as regular before, and the unknown number had not called in a few days. Tiffany sent a text saying that she would be in town this weekend and that everyone is ready to get out and kick it. Saturday rolled around, and the whole week had been very chill. Nothing had changed in Treys' patterns. He was still being the king of his castle and treating his wife like gold. It seemed that all was well, and that Katrina had worried over something trivial. Now the thought of going through all of that trouble to catch Trey was for nothing.

Later on that night, she hooked up with the girls, and they were having a blast, dancing and knocking back a few long islands. The dance club was packed, and everyone was having a good time. Katrina and Tiffany took a break from dancing and went to the bar to get drinks for everybody in their group.

As they waited on their drinks, they faced each other, talking and laughing. Katrina felt a hand squeeze her around her waist. She turned around and standing there was a tall, handsome man. He looked around and noticed Katrina staring at him, so he offered to buy her a drink. She smiled and politely declined the offer and told the man she was married. The man had a look of confusion on his face as he checked her out. Katrina turned back around, raising her eyebrows at Tiffany shaking her head. Next, she felt a gentle kiss on her neck, and it almost took her to her knees. She turned around and told the man to please stop and that what he did was so disrespectful. He stared at her with a look of confusion. Tiffany told her she was tripping. She grabbed Katrina by the shoulders and turned her back around, facing her.

Tiffany told Katrina that she'd had enough to drink, and she needed to stop acting crazy. All of a sudden, Katrina felt her ass being squeezed and groped all over! She turned around without hesitation and slapped the man. In an uproar yelling and cursing, she wanted to call the police for sexual harassment on this man, causing a scene. Tiffany and her friends tried to calm her down and told Katrina that the guy didn't do anything to her!

They walked her to the car for some fresh air and to cool down. As she looked for the keys to get in her car, she tried to call Trey to tell him what happened, but he didn't pick up the phone. She got in the car, and as she was sitting there trying to gather her composure, she got a sexual sensation from penetration. She immediately tried to call her husband but got no answer again. As her friends were sitting and leaning on the car, she started it and put it in drive. Her friends looked around, confused because she almost ran over a few toes.

"Girl, what are you doing with your drunk ass?" Tiffany said.

Katrina rolled down the window and said, "I gotta get home now. I have an emergency. I'll catch up with y'all another day."

Katrina sped off. Tiffany being the friend she was, hopped in her car and followed Katrina. As Katrina pulled up to the house, Tiffany pulled up right behind her, trying to stop her and find out what was going on!

"I called this motherfucker, and he didn't pick up," Katrina said. "Remember the witch doctor I told you about and what he did to me? I just got that feeling, and now Trey is not answering his phone. I'm about to act a straight fool when I get in here."

"Are you serious?" Tiffany sighed. "Well, if the bitch still in there, we about to send her ass to the med in critical condition."

As they entered the house, Trey had his robe on and was up cooking a late-night snack. Katrina stormed in, exclaiming,

"Where she at??"

"What in the hell are you talking about?" Trey said. "Baby, you need to stop drinking, I see. Tiffany, what is going on?"

"I don't know, Trey, you tell us. Just tell the truth! Trey, if you got somebody in here, we can settle this now," Tiffany replied.

"Man, if I knew y'all were gonna drink and come back acting like this, she would have never been able to leave," Trey replied.

"Who are you to tell me when I can and can't leave? Where is she, Trey?" Katrina yelled.

"How about checking all over the house y'all damn selves. You should know better, baby. Me, cheat on you?"

"You are tripping big time, but imma let you have this one because ain't no telling what all y'all were talking about that got you all hyped up. I'm going to bed. Goodnight."

"Tiffany, lock the door on your way out," Trey replied. As Trey walked off, Katrina yelled at him to come back and tell the truth. Tiffany grabbed her arm and tried to calm her down.

"Katrina, chill out. This man ain't got nobody here! Are you sure you felt something?" Tiffany asked.

"Well, why didn't he answer the phone?" Katrina said.

"I don't know. Hell, we didn't ask him that. We came in yelling and ready to fight."

"Damn, girl you right, but I know what I felt, and he should have answered the damn phone. If he had somebody, he would be acting weird, and he isn't. Damn, I look so stupid."

"For real, girl, we do," Tiffany replied. "You know you my girl, but this time we probably went a little far. It'll be all good in the morning."

"When ya'll wake up, just blame it on the alcohol and tell him you just got worried from listening to them other bitches' problems. He'll forgive you, and all will be well."

"You're right, girl." Katrina agreed. "I'm going to apologize and sleep on the couch. Maybe I'm tripping. But maybe I'm not though. If it's meant for me to catch him, I will, right?"

"That's right, what's done in the dark will come to light," Tiffany assured her.

So the night passed by, and in the morning, they both woke up around the same time. It seemed as if they both knew the other wanted to talk about what happened. Katrina woke up and went straight to the bathroom to freshen up and brush her teeth. Trey was sitting on the side of the bed when she walked back into the room.

"Good morning," Trey said.

"Good morning," Katrina replied (as she walked to the bathroom and then back out of it) "Baby, let me say this first I'm so sorry."

Trey replied, "Babe, you were *on* one last night. What gave you the idea that I was cheating on you? Do you believe I would cheat on you? What signs have I given you to make you feel like that? You should know me better than that baby."

"Baby, I do, and I'm sorry. You haven't done anything that's out of the ordinary, and I know that you're a good man." Katrina replied. "I guess I can just imagine women throwing themselves at you now."

"I can't lie, baby they do try to get at me, but just like I was in high school, I only have eyes for one and one only, you."

They kissed and made up and began to get ready to part ways for work. Katrina truly knew that Trey loved her.

CHAPTER ELEVEN

The 2nd Feeling

Katrina was at work on her computer, looking over a few accounts. She sipped her coffee and tried to get over her little hangover. All of a sudden, she got a weird feeling of lips on her neck. She shook her head to try and throw the image of Trey doing something crazy out of her mind. She took a deep breath, and as she exhaled, the intensity of the kiss sparked passion throughout all of her veins. As she continued to shake her head and close her eyes to the voice of Dr. Oni in her head, repeating the words, "you will feel the sexual pleasures of your true love when he is in the act."

The kisses were no longer on her neck but now have found their way to her breasts. She sat back in awe, feeling paranoid of people looking through the open door of her office. Realizing that, Katrina tried to gain her composure and just let it happen. Although her fists were clenched in rage and anger, the sexual intercourse was relaxing and very pleasurable.

Deeply breathing, she tried to control her exhales as she began having an orgasm. Tears started to fall down her eyes, and she reached for the phone to call her husband to see what he was up to. No answer. So she immediately dialed the number to her friend Tiffany.

Tiffany answered, "Hey boo, what's up?"

"That feeling I told you about happened again, and this time I'm not drunk, plus I am at work," Katrina replied.

"Describe the feelings to me."

"I don't think you would believe me if I told you..."

"Just tell me so that I can have some kind of idea if it's all in your mind or something..."

"Tiff, I know it's not in my mind. This time I sat back and let it happen..."

"Let what happen?"

"Ok, look, I just had a full-on orgasm. My juices are flowing down my legs as we speak, and the thing that bothers me the most is that it's been a while since Trey has made me cum like this. I mean, he ain't bad in bed."

"He used to drive my body like a Cadillac, but lately, it has been so routine that sometimes I fake the irregular period move not to have sex. The romance is not there like it was, but he still tries. It's the normal sex and scheduled times that are getting old..."

"You had an orgasm at work?! Did you moan, scream, or hell, did you even say his name girl?" Tiffany asked jokingly.

"Why are you taking this for a joke? No, I just sat back and let it happen because I felt like people were watching me. I couldn't get up to close the door in time to enjoy it. Plus, I didn't want to enjoy it knowing where it was coming from."

"That couldn't have been me. I would have been trying to ride that chair girl," Tiffany laughed.

"It sounds like you're making fun of me. Imma call you back when you stop playing."

"I'm not playing, so what are you going to do now?"

I'm about to ask my boss for an early lunch and pop up on him at work."

"Please don't act no fool. Call me before you start to blow up if you have to."

"Ok, imma let you know how this goes."

Katrina left her office and headed to her husband's workplace. She called his office phone, no answer. So she called his cell phone, and he picked it up.

Trey answered, "What's up, baby?"

"What are you doing?"

"I'm at work. Why, what's up?"

"I just called your office phone, and you didn't pick up. You sure you at work? I'm outside your office and about to come in. I want to have lunch with you today."

"Ok, that's unusual, but give me about 10 mins, and I'll be ready. I'll come outside to you. Where do you want to go?"

"Well, I want to come in and wait in your office until you get ready. Tell your receptionist to unlock the front door."

"I said, give me 10 mins I will be out in a few.

"Why can't I come in? Who are you screwing now, your receptionist?"

"What is your damn problem? You said you came to have lunch, but you are on some other mess. I'm coming out right now to let you in!"

Katrina got out of her car to go into the building. Trey met her at the door with a face of disapproval. Katrina walked past the receptionist desk only to see there was no one there. So in her mind, the receptionist was around here somewhere, and he was trying to give her time to get dressed.

Katrina stormed in, "Where is your receptionist?"
Out of the men's bathroom walks a charming-looking man.

"Speaking of the devil, there he is. He was using the restroom when you called, and I didn't know how long he would be in there. Come into my office. We need to talk." Trey responded.

Katrina was now thinking that her husband was going to tell her that he was gay. As they walked into his office, she heard people talking on the phone. Trey gave her the silent signal by placing his finger over his lips so that he could get back to the phone conference and discussion he was having before she showed up. He unmuted the phone and asked the party to excuse his absence and that he would like to continue with their conversation. Katrina looked at him and tried to signal that she would just come back after realizing he was on the phone this whole time.

Feeling so stupid, she stood up and started walking towards the door. Trey held his hand up in a pausing position and wrapped up the conversation he was having on the phone.

"Babe, I missed your call because I was on the phone with a client and other colleagues going over a case. Now you bum rush me as if I had someone in here. What is your deal?" Trey said.

"I have no deal," Katrina replied. "I just wanted to come to your office and see my baby at work. What's wrong with me doing that?"

"Ok, so then what was up with you accusing me of sexing my receptionist? I'm not gay, and I don't appreciate you coming to the office like this lying."

"I'm not accusing you of anything. I just made a joke Trey; dang you all in your feelings! Do you still want to go with me for lunch? I only got 15 minutes or so. You made me wait half of my break time."

"Well, the nearest place to eat something good is about ten minutes away, or we can grab some gas station snack boxes?"

"Naw, I'm good," Katrina said. "I don't want food from the gas station."

"I'll just go to the sub shop on the way back to work. It's close to my job. Imma see you later after work. I love you!"

On her way back to work, she called Tiffany and told her what went down and how she thought for a minute he was going to come out of the closet on her! They both cracked up laughing.

CHAPTER TWELVE
The Gift or The Curse

"Girl, I gotta call that doctor back and let him know he didn't do nothing but give me sexual pleasure and that he needs to remove this spell so I can stop tripping," Katrina told Tiffany.

"Why would you do that after you told me how good it was? You said Trey don't rock your body like he used to. If I were you, I would keep it and enjoy it to the fullest! What's that doctor's name and number? Hell, I want him to do that to me!"

"You right, girl. I might as well keep it," Katrina replied halfheartedly.

This went on for months, and when she got the feeling, she just sat back and enjoyed it no matter where she was. Tiffany called Katrina and asked her for the number again. Tiffany said that she must have given her the wrong number because it was no longer in service. Katrina laughed and told her how out of luck she was and that she should have called *months* ago. "

"Why are you just *now* calling the number? I gave it to you a while ago," Katrina asked.

"Well, my man done hit his sexual peak, and I need it more now. He can't keep up with me, and I'm getting bored with him. I don't want to cheat on him, so I need this," Tiffany replied. They tried to do a quick search on Dr. Oni, and he no longer had a business page or online ads.

* * *

Time passed, and things seemed to be going really well for Katrina and Trey. No more accusations, no arguing about Trey not answering his phone in front of her, and no more popping up at his job to try to catch him. That suddenly changed when one of Katrina and Tiffany's friends caught Trey out having lunch with a very beautiful woman. So like all women do, they called and talked about what they saw. Katrina wanted to know what this chick looked like more than anything so that she could think about who it could be. She was puzzled but now more confused than ever.

She contemplated how to talk to Trey about it without accusing or making assumptions. Later that evening, they both were off of work and at home chilling. While they prepared dinner together, Katrina found a way to bring this woman up.

"So today I got a call saying you were with a very beautiful woman. I'm not accusing you, but what's that about?" Katrina asked.

"First off, you got people spying on me?" Trey replied.

"Boy please, you know this is a small town, and everybody sees everything. It just got back to me, and I guess they were telling me as if I would get jealous."

"Well, you don't have to be jealous. It's an old colleague of mine. We had a case today and bumped into each other. So we grabbed a bite to eat on her way out of town. It meant nothing, and that's probably the last time I'll ever see her," Trey said.

"Ok Trey, don't get your head busted. It better be the last time."

"Baby, if she ever comes back, I want you to meet her, so you will know who she is and know that nothing is going on," Trey said.

Katrina shrugged the conversation to the side and acted like it meant nothing to her. It was her way to show Trey she wasn't going to trip on him and go back to the thought of anything negative.

* * *

A few weeks passed by, and she didn't get the orgasmic feelings anymore. It boggled her mind as she tried to figure out why. She called Tiffany and told her what was going.

"What are you doing? You got time to talk?"

"I'm at work chilling, so yeah, I got time. What's up?" Tiffany replied.

"I lost the gift, Tiff. It's gone, and I don't know what happened," Katrina told her.

"When did this happen?"

"A few weeks ago."

"Maybe it's a phase or a mood you been in or something. It will probably come back."

"I thought the same thing, and somehow I feel something different about it. I miss it, but I don't," Katrina said.

"Don't take what I say seriously, but what if the woman our friend saw Trey with broke up with him or something, and what you were feeling was them? That may be a little out there, but I don't know what else it could have been," Tiffany suggested.

"That's the only thing that didn't cross my mind. How could I have been so blind this time not to see it? I have tried to catch him numerous times and never could. But now, all of a sudden, it stopped. When I asked him about that woman he said, that was probably the last time he would ever see her, and if she ever did come back to town, he would let me meet her. That bold motherfucker!"

"I probably shouldn't have said that to you. Don't feel like he got one over on you. I'm just talking. Don't take me seriously," Tiffany replied.

"I ain't saying nothing. Imma give him the chance to come clean. I might hint around about it and see what other clues I can get out of him to confirm my suspicion," Katrina concluded.

CHAPTER THIRTEEN
The Set-Up

Katrina got home before Trey to set up the house for some romantic action. Trey got home to a dark setting. The lights were off, and candles were lit. In the air was the sweet perfume he loves his wife to wear.

"Baby, what's going on in here?"

Katrina yelled from a distance, "I'm in the bathroom, baby come in here. I have your bath water ready, my king."

He walked up the stairs and into the bathroom.

"Oh man, what is it now? I've already married you, are you finally pregnant? Trey jokingly replied.

"What do you mean finally? You better not be plotting on me boy. Anyways no, I am not pregnant. I just wanted to do something nice for you, that's all. Let's talk. It has been far too long since we had a conversation with each other about any and everything." As Trey got undressed and entered the soothing water, Katrina shared a lot of small talk leading up to what she really wanted to know.

"Trey baby, what are some things that I could improve on that would make our marriage stronger?"

"Well, I don't know. I would seriously have to think about that because you are everything I want and need."

"Naw, don't give me that sweet man I married. I want your brutal honesty. I want you to get everything off of your chest. Trey, I want you to be real with me. Let's forget about the fact that I'm your wife. Right now, I'm your friend, and you are talking to me about what your wife could start and stop doing that would make things easier for you."

"Where is this coming from? Trey replied. "I'll tell you what. I would open up more if you told me what it is *you* want and need.

"Ok, for one, I hate when you blow me off as if my concerns don't matter to you," Katrina told him.

"I didn't know I was blowing you off like that. Tell me what I blew you off about."

"Well, what about that strange number that kept calling you? I asked you about it, and you told me it was nothing. Your words to me were to "let it go" as if I would be ok with that."

"Well, I still stand firm on that! Trey exclaimed. "Ok, my turn, recently your behavior has changed.

"My behavior?"

"Yes, your behavior. You have been coming to my job sporadically with no justification. You act as if I don't know you are trying to catch me cheating."

"Well, are you?" Katrina asked him.

"No, I am not, and I don't like this game. My vows to you are being questioned, and I will be damned if I let you. We were supposed to tell each other what we didn't like and make the marriage better. What are we doing?" Trey replied.

"I am telling you what it is I don't like. I don't like being lied to and cheated on! So the friend you saw weeks back, what's really going on? How many times have you seen her? Katrina asked.

"Ok, now I see what this is about. Yes, I saw her more than one time. I think I saw her 5 or 6 times." Trey answered.

"Did you go out each time?" Katrina asked.

"Yes, I had lunch with her, but only once have I had lunch with her *alone*. Our other colleagues tagged along most of the time."

"The reason we were alone last time was only due to people canceling at the last minute. As I said before, we were working on a large class action lawsuit, and she was one of the team members for the company."

"Well, how long was she here for, and why did you keep this from me?" Katrina replied.

"Because I knew you wouldn't like it, and it would cause a split in the house like it is now. I don't have an answer on how long she had been here because I wasn't keeping up with all that. She is gone now, and I will probably never see or talk to her again. Plus, I don't have her number to stay in contact."

"See, that answer may suit you, but I'm still not satisfied. And again, you are blowing me off and have yet to give me the answer I deserve to hear." Katrina replied.

"Just know I don't mix business with pleasure. You are my wife, my partner in marriage, not my coworker, and not some random person outside our home."

"What home?" Katrina replied.

Trey got up from the tub, wrapped a towel around himself, and walked out of the bathroom, leaving Katrina there sitting on the tub. As she was contemplating what just happened, Trey prepared for bed. The two still went to bed together but with lots of space between them. Later that night, Trey burned with passion and refused to go to sleep mad and not make his wife feel satisfied.

Trey woke Katrina up by ripping her panties off. As she tried to complain and make an argument, he quickly places his fingers over her lips as his tongue speaks to her body. Then to her neck and breast, down her stomach, and between her legs. As he gently nibbled between her thigh, Katrina conformed. As the sighs of her breath got deeper and more exaggerated, it confirmed she was willing. Trey was unleashing the freak. Katrina quickly thought about the type of orgasm she got off of the "gift." Now, this had become a test of routine and similarities. During the times she was sexually satisfied by the "gift," the sensations are like being licked all over from head to toe. She noticed that trey was not just all over her body with his tongue but was in a few places he normally didn't go. This was different but still good to her.

Trey manhandled her in a way that was physically enthralling, and he easily flipped her over. As he bit her, she could feel how intensely he wanted to be inside of her. After he had entered her, he kissed her on the back of her neck, softly grabbed her throat, and he whispered in her ear, "who's pussy is this"?

Katrina moaned like never before, hesitant to answer. Trey asked again, "who's pussy is this" as he pushed deeper inside of her. She finally answered, saying his name over and over. Although she fell into a submissive state, something was still missing. It was the kissing, sucking of her lips, and the feeling of arms wrapped around her torso tightly with the sense of protection from the "gift" that was missing. In Trey's mind, he gave Katrina the best sex ever. In Katrina's mind, he forgot to make love to her.

There was a slight difference in the feelings she got, but she was undeniably pleased by Trey. While you would think this would put Katrina's mind at ease, she was now convinced Trey had been cheating. She felt this way because his sex was not routine but *better*. Almost as if another woman had showed him how to please the body.

A few days passed by, and there was a certain stillness in the air. It seemed that trying to talk it out was no longer on the table for Katrina. The awkwardness of resolution is what made the air too thin to share.

CHAPTER FOURTEEN

Bad Things, Good Timing

Katrina was at work, getting ready for her morning meeting to discuss numbers with her boss and fellow employees, when her office phone rang. With a puzzled look, wondering who it could be, she answered. It was the sound of a woman on the other end.

"Hello, Katrina?"

"Yes, this is Katrina. Who am I talking to?"

"This is Mya, and I'm calling on behalf of Trey."

"Trey? Wait a minute, who is this again, and how do you know my husband?"

"I'm an old friend of Trey's, and we recently worked on a case together."

"Oh, ok, so why are you calling me? How did you get my number?" Katrina asked.

"Well, Trey called me a few days ago and told me of your concerns. So I wanted to reach out to you and let you know nothing happened."

"We went to lunch a few times, and that was it. Trey is a special man, and I know he loves you," Mya said.

"Ok, thank you, but did you say Trey called you? Did you exchange numbers with him?"

"No, we didn't exchange numbers. I still have the same number since college. I am not trying to be messy, but I used to date Trey in college, and he probably still had my number saved. That doesn't mean anything. I just called to tell you that Trey is a great man." Mya answered.

"Ok, well I have to get back to work, and I will save your number in case I need a lawyer," Katrina said sarcastically.

"Sure, keep it if you ever want to talk again. I'll be around," Mya concluded.

They both hung up, and now Katrina was furious. Trey never told her that this woman was an ex, plus he said he didn't have her number. Lies on top of secrets made for a very angry woman. As usual, bad news always has good timing. This mentally threw Katrina off focus and into a sunken place. Attending the morning meeting was not on her mind at all.

She wanted to go home and fight Trey with every inch of her being, but she sat in her chair dazed. Her thoughts went to the many conversations she and her friends talked about and then to Trey and his secrets. Katrina stared for hours at an empty spot on the wall. Then in walked her boss wondering if everything was ok.

"Yes, I just had a rough start to my day, but nothing a little aspirin can't fix," Katrina told him.

"Oh, I see. I've had many of those nights. Hangover, right?"

"You can call it that, just a little bit too much girl talk (with her hand on her head). What did I miss?"

"You didn't miss much really, the usual. Do you have your numbers for today? I can grab them really quick and let you get a little shut eye if needed," he replied.

"I will email you my documents right now, and I'll be ok. I just need a second to breathe."

* * *

Katrina called her mom for some advice.

"Momma, I need a big favor from you."

"Ok baby, what do you need? Do you want me to get your daddy really quick to help as well?" her mom Valerie replied.

"No ma'am, it's actually just advice and truths I need from you right now."

"Ok honey, tell me what you got. I'll answer to the best of my ability," her mom replied.

"Has dad ever cheated on you?"

"Yes!"

"What?! I was not expecting that at all!"

"Well, you asked for the truth, and there it is. Your dad cheated on me twice. The crazy thing is I knew when he did it. I just had a feeling in my bones."

"Momma, I did not know that! How did you handle it?"

"Well, I started by shutting him out completely. I made nothing a part of my day when it came to him! Meaning I stopped talking to him and cut sex off from him. He didn't even realize till months later when he tried to kiss me. I backed up and continued to wash dishes as a part of my normal routine."

"Why didn't you leave him?"

"Baby, you loved your daddy so much I couldn't dream of taking you away, as much as I hurt. I was a stay-at-home mom with nothing to my name nor any skill set that would allow me to survive without him."

With tears in her eyes, Katrina said, "Momma you can live with me now. You don't have to go through that anymore. I'm so done with men and their shit. Do you want to come stay with me? You don't have to worry about money."

"It's okay now. Me and your father are better now than ever!"

"Huh, I don't understand?"

"The day your father realized I knew about it, and how hurt I was... he came clean to me. I mean, he just laid it all out there. That was the first time I saw Joe cry. That was on your 4th birthday. You blew out your candles, but I made the wish. We talked for hours upon hours. He sat there listening to me cry and curse him up and down. Joe knew there was nothing to say that could make me forgive him in an instant. From that day, he worked hard to bring a smile back to my face."

"Those are the days you saw, the effort your dad made to make me his number one priority. I couldn't imagine a better love than this. It took time *and* work."

"Why are you just now telling me this? You didn't think I could handle it?" Katrina asked.

"What you see now, the happiness and how a man is supposed to treat his woman is what I wanted you to see. Not the bad and the unfaithfulness, but how it could be for *you*. People make mistakes all the time but how they turn it around is the value of lessons learned."

"So, you just forgave dad like that, no more worrying if he would do it again or just try to hide it better? Did any of the chicks he cheated with say anything to you?" Katrina asked her mom.

"Honestly, not a day went by that I didn't assume he was still cheating, and not a day went by that he didn't try to show me how truly sorry he was. Katrina, where is this coming from?"

"I think Trey is cheating on me. I got proof, but I haven't actually caught him in the act of doing it. Just a few lies and secrets that he has."

"What does your gut say? Better yet, what does your spirit tell you?"

"I'm still confused because his routine is the same, and he treats me the same. I don't want to forgive him. But if he tells the truth and allows me the chance to heal then maybe I could let this blow over and not continue to punish him for it."

"I don't want you to feel like you must forgive and stay with him because of my story. You are a way stronger person than I could have ever imagined being. I want you to do what your heart tells you. Although no man is perfect, no woman deserves to be cheated on. It's up to you, and I support whatever decision you make."

"The last thing I want to ask you is, have you ever cheated back? Didn't you feel deserving of it?"

"There were a few men who constantly tried to steal me from your father, but when I think of what true forgiveness is, the idea never became a reality."

"Katrina, do you know the saying, forgive and forget? Do you know what that means? It means to forgive the person for what they did and try to forget about it." her mom said.

"That's the hard part. I don't think I would ever forget."

"So it means to forgive. You have that part right. But to forget is not the actual thing of forgetting what happened. It's the ability to forget the pain it caused you when you think of what happened. Put it like this. Your favorite dog died. You would cry that day and probably a few weeks after. Time would continue to pass, but you would no longer cry. You would still remember the dog on different occasions. You may see a dog that looked like the one you had. You may see people doing things with their dog you used to do with yours. In the end, you would remember your dog from time to time and even how it died, but no longer dwell in the past with hurt feelings. Just think about that," her mom concluded.

They get off the phone, and Katrina went back to thinking about what she wanted to do. This decision was big, especially after hearing her mom's side to a cheating man. The forgiveness she showed and the restraint to stay faithful to her marriage amazed her. Katrina didn't think she had that type of strength, and she refused to go through another cheating relationship and wait too long to get out of it. Katrina went home and asked Trey to talk with her.

* * *

"Tell me what's on your mind," Trey started.

"I want out. I'm done. I can't deal with you and your lies." Katrina replied.

"My lies! You want out? What in the hell is going on? I have done nothing but been good to you, and now you want out? This is bullshit! What if I say no?"

"You can say what you want, but I just can't do this anymore."

"Baby, please don't do this to me. I'll do whatever it takes!"

"So did you date Mya when y'all were in college?"

"Yes, but it didn't last long at all! She was not the one for me, and I knew that immediately after we tried dating. We became way better friends than lovers."

"Yeah yeah, how did you get her number? You told me you didn't have her number."

"I didn't remember having her number. It's been so long since I talked to her and who would have thought she would have the same number since freshman year of college! Plus, I called her office to get in touch with her, and her intern gave me her cell phone number. I realized I had it when she started calling out the numbers."

"That sounds like bull. Why were you trying to reach out to her in the first place?"

"After you asked me, I wanted to have her talk to you. So she could tell you nothing was going on with us."

"She was probably lying because she called me and told me that y'all went out a few times since she was here. Then she was the one who told me that you and her used to date. You told me that you went with other people the times y'all grabbed food. She made it seem like it was personal. Then proceeded to tell me how great of a man you are...!"

"So she did call you! I was the one who asked for her to do that. Only to prove my innocence about something you should know better than--"

"Do *not* tell me what I should know better than. You should have known better than to go out with her without telling me. Then on top of that, you lied. I need space!"

"Baby, I am so sorry! I would never do that again! This was so harmless, and now you make it this big. Come on, baby please?!"

"Trey, just leave and give me some time to think. I'll get back to you with my answer in a few days."

CHAPTER FIFTEEN

Jackson Amorette

Trey and Katrina split up for a few days, and it made Trey absolutely sick. Katrina stuck to her guns and her beliefs. She told Trey she emotionally checked out and no longer thought she had what it took to make it work. She felt as if she would never be able to forgive him after knowing how Dallas did her in college. She felt that Trey should have known better. Katrina served Trey divorce papers, but he was in denial of calling it quits. Trey tried every day to get his woman back but failed miserably because at this point, she wouldn't budge. She talked to her mom and friend Tiffany and they both felt that she was doing the right thing.

* * *

One day while Katrina was at work, a sharply dressed man came into the bank. He was looking to set up an account with a large amount of cash, and a normal teller couldn't assist him. Katrina was the only one on duty at the time that could open this type of account.

This man was the picture-perfect dream guy. His charm, his smile, the way he smelled, his style, his build, his eyes, and hell, even his walk was something special. Katrina saw all of that and was *very* willing to help him. He sat down and introduced himself as Jackson Amorette. They began to talk, and man, did they have the best conversation. Jackson had all the right words to say, and the way he said them was just so mesmerizing.

"Thank you for helping me out. I have been to other banks, and the amount I have to set up an account exceeds the maximum limit," Jackson told her.

"No problem, glad that we can help you. If you don't mind me asking, what is it you do that requires you to have all this money on you at one time?" Katrina replied.

"I own a construction company, Stone Constructions that I built from the ground up. The name came from my father, and it was my childhood nickname. Guessing my head must have been hard as a rock."

"So, you carry around this much money because of construction? I am in the wrong business, for real. You need an accountant?" Katrina laughed.

"Truth be told, one of my truckers was badly hurt in an accident from using faulty equipment and won a large settlement. He has been working for me for about six years now, and I know the guy personally. His lifestyle and the company he keeps around him will drain him dry of his money. He came to me and wanted me to handle things as far as his bills go. He knows that I have his best interest in mind and no need for his money."

When Katrina heard this, it melted her heart. She compared this man to her father. It seemed like every man she met, Mr. Joe was who she measured them by. Even though she didn't know a lot about Jackson, he peaked her interest, and she wanted to learn more. Of course, this would require more time spent with him in a dating manner, and Katrina didn't know if she was ready for all that. She also knew that she didn't want to miss out on the chance of getting to know this man.

As her mind was racing with these thoughts, the last thing she needed was for him to ask her out. She would hate to tell him no, but deep down, she wanted him to ask her. Katrina and Jackson went through the paperwork and finished up the account setup.

They both rose from their chairs and told each other how much they appreciated the conversation and business transaction. Jackson reached across Katrina's desk to shake her hand.

"Mrs. Katrina, it has been a pleasure. I hope I'm not crossing the line when I say that you are truly beautiful and that your husband is a lucky man," as he is still holding her hand.

Without hesitation, Katrina replied, "I'm currently going through a divorce."

"Oh, well, I'm sorry to hear that. I don't know much about you, but I find it hard to believe that a man is willing to lose you without a fight. So why do you still wear the ring? Is he fighting hard enough to make you keep that on?"

"I have my reasons, but mainly to keep men away (as they chuckle at what she said). I just meet so many dogs out here, that I keep my shield up. Many try, but all fail because they lack respect nowadays," she replied.

"I mean no harm or disrespect. I am simply thrown back by your beauty, your intelligence, and your ability to conduct business. To have all three is the rarest thing I've ever seen!"

"Thank you so much, you are very kind. So, what's your angle Sir?" Katrina asked him.

"My angle? What do you mean?" Jackson replied.

"Yes, your angle! You have been holding my hand ever since we stood up, and now you are saying all of these things."

"Truth be told, I want to take you to dinner. I respect you and your ex-husband to be, but if I walk out of here without at least trying. I would hate myself for days, maybe even weeks. I'll let go of your hand if you say yes."

"Mr. Jackson, how many women have you said this to?"

"If I have, I don't remember. But I do mean what I say right now," Jackson answered.

"Oh, ok. Just so you will let go of my hand, YES, I'll go out with you. But you better know how to treat a woman. I require and expect the best, so just know I will be blunt if you let me down." Katrina told him.

* * *

Time went by, and they both had been enjoying each other. Five dates in, and Jackson had not disappointed. Katrina decided she wanted to do something different.

She wanted to let Jackson know that she liked *him* and not his money. So she planned an evening with him in the park. No money needed, just walking and talking. As the sun set, they found a bench to enjoy the view. There were a couple of benches to choose from, but Katrina took him to the one she and Trey normally sat at. It had the best view of the park lake, and the sunset was so beautiful from there.

CHAPTER SIXTEEN

Frustration

As they sat, Katrina laid in Jackson's lap and talked about the fun she has had with him these past few weeks. While lying there, she heard a car pull up. She raised her head in curiosity to see who was getting out of it. It was a taxi dropping off two individuals. She stared in that direction for no apparent reason, but to be nosey. It was Trey and another woman exiting the vehicle! She quickly jumped up and wanted to get out of there immediately.

"What's wrong, babe?" Jackson asked.

"Nothing really; I just want to leave."

Jackson looked over and saw who Katrina was looking at.

"Is that him?"

"Him who?"

"We passed the stage of hiding things, and I'm a big boy. I can handle it," Jackson replied.

"Yes, that's him, and it irks my nerves that he is here. He knows I love this spot."

"And on top of all that, he brings another woman here. Jackson, please call a taxi, and let's get out of here," Katrina answered with a look of sadness and frustration on her face.

Jackson called for the same taxi that had just dropped off Trey and the other woman. As the taxi was looping around to come to pick them up, Trey looked over to see Jackson comforting Katrina as they walked away from the park bench to meet the taxi as it arrived. Trey yelled Katrina's name loudly as he tried to get her attention. He called her name repeatedly as he started walking towards them, completely forgetting about the other woman as though she was never there. Jackson stuck his hand out in a stopping motion towards Trey, signaling him not to come over there. The taxi pulled up, and they got in, with Trey still walking towards the car.

"Where to?" the driver asked as Jackson looked down at Katrina.

"Take me to your house please. I don't want to go home in case he tries to pop up at my door."

Jackson gave the address to the cab driver as they pulled off. Once they arrived at Jackson's estate, Katrina and Jackson walked to the door.

Before they could get in the house, Katrina turned to him, blocking the doorway, and started kissing him. Struggling to get the key in the door, Jackson was now going with the flow. They entered the house, made it to the couch, and were still passionately kissing. Jackson pulled back.

"I want you bad, but not like this. You are just in a vulnerable state right now, and I don't want to take advantage of the situation."

"I'm a big girl. I know what I'm doing Jackson. Right now, I just want you inside of me. Please don't take this away from me."

Jackson started back kissing her, ripping her shirt off, and kissing her neck. Katrina reached down Jackson's pants only to find out Jackson was not ready to make this happen.

"What's going on Jackson?"

"Just give me a minute to get started."

"Am I turning you off? Do you not want me?"

"With every bone in my body, I do. I'm getting there. Just give me a minute to take care of you first! I will not disappoint."

They start back going at it, and still, Jackson is unable to get an erection. Katrina backed up and started putting her clothes back on, stating that this was a mistake.

"Take me home Jackson. It's obvious that you don't want me."

"Wow, really? Just like that, you want to go home. I truly don't know what's going on. Something just doesn't feel right."

"Maybe another day, but right now, I just want to go home and not be bothered."

"You really bout to act like that? I have been nothing but good and understanding to you. Now you want to leave that bad and not be bothered? You can just catch an Uber. I'm not leaving my house again tonight."

"Cool, I'm going to wait outside for my ride. I don't need to be in here, *clearly*."

She put back on her clothes as she and Jackson were short with words and didn't give each other eye contact.

* * *

The next day she got to work, and the first thing she did was call Tiffany.

"Tiff, you know I'm not a whore, right?"

"Girl, what in the world are you talking about?"

"Nothing, I was just asking you because I was about to let Jackson get some last night, but his dick didn't work."

"You mean to tell me that fine-ass man dick didn't work?!"

"Well, he seemed to be more concerned about my situation than sexing me."

"What situation?"

"We saw Trey getting out of a taxi with another woman at the park. So I had Jackson call for that same taxi. I wanted Trey to see me get in the car with Jackson. When Trey saw me, he started screaming my name and coming towards us. Jackson was like, hold up, don't walk towards us, and we got in the car!"

"What did Trey do? Did he stop walking?"

"We left before he got there. I told Jackson to take me to his house. That's what I really called you about."

"You went to his house?"

"I'm still mad he couldn't get it up. I was like, what the hell. Just when I needed it most, he couldn't perform."

"He must have wanted it so bad, girl. I had a man do me the same way. Don't trip. It happens to the best of them."

"Well, the killer part is he put me out of his house!"

"Aw hell naw, where do he stay? Let's pull up on him and bust a window or something."

"He didn't really put me out per se, but when I got up and started putting my clothes back on, I asked him to take me home. He was like no, catch an Uber. So I left his house and waited outside.

"Has he tried to call you?"

"Not at all. Well, at least not today."

"I probably would have put you out too. You just jumped up and asked to go home without a good reason. You cold-blooded girl!"

"Was I wrong for that? Should I call him and apologize?

"Do you like him, or are you still in love with Trey?"

"I really don't know. Trey cheated on me, and I just wanted him to see me with another man. I was letting him know that I would be just fine without him. After seeing him chase after me, I could see the pain in his eyes. Still, he came there with another woman."

He just left her standing there. I just started thinking about what would have happened if Jackson and I *did* have sex. Right now, I just don't know.

"Can't help you with that one. Never been in that situation."

"I don't know anymore. After seeing him with another woman, it's like he doesn't exist anymore because he was so quick to move on."

"But you are doing the same thing girl. You asked him for a divorce. What else is he supposed to do? You don't answer his calls anymore; when you see him you are mean, and you put him out of y'all house!"

"I know, I know. But I *didn't* cheat on him, and I don't think I can forgive him."

Just as Katrina and Tiffany ended their conversation, an employee who works with Katrina walked into her office, informing her that Trey was out in the waiting area for her. Katrina told her coworker to get him. Trey walked into the office with a sad and exhausted look on his face.

"Trey, I don't know what it is that you want, but I don't have much time, so please make this quick."

"Katrina, baby, it's been so hard for me to sleep ever since you told me you wanted a divorce. That was almost three months ago, and just a few weeks ago, I thought I was going to snap and lose it."

"I would not wish the way I feel on my worst enemy, but last night I could have died, and all I could think about is if you would have cared. After seeing you with that man, I'm beginning to think that you're over me and ready to move on with your life--"

"Trey, I really don't have time for this. You cheated on me first, and I don't know what else you want me to do. Just sign the divorce papers, you keep what you had, and I keep what I had. It's that simple Trey. Let's not make this hard."

"I have *never* cheated on you, and you know how much I love you. But I didn't come here to argue about this. Every day I wreck my brain thinking of what I did to make you feel this way. I know I could have been more honest about meeting up with that old colleague for lunch. I just didn't think it would go this far. But what else did I do that made you call it quits?"

"Trey, you know what you did, and you want to be all in your feelings when you see me with somebody else. Now you know how it feels, plus who was the girl you were with last night? See, you just got caught up again, and now you wanna beg me back?"

"Caught up again? I met that woman in a shared taxi. We just so happened to be going in the same direction."

"I was going to the park to clear my head and remember the times we shared there. I have been there like every night, hoping that I would bump into you. Never in my mind did I see you being there with another man. Did you have sex with him?"

"That's none of your business anymore. How does it feel to know someone you trusted could do you that way?"

"I woke up this morning to pray about things. I saw God as the last option to win your heart back because I just knew this would last forever. I really believed that, but the answer I got this morning was not what I wanted or needed. I am here to say yes to the divorce. I will not fight with you. Here are the forms signed and ready for whatever else you want to do. I gave you my heart, and now I will give you everything else you want."

"Can we have this done by Friday? Today is Monday, so that gives you a few days to go ahead and make this final," Trey asked.

"Thank you, now go enjoy your old colleague or other women you might have," Katrina replied.

"I don't want her or anybody else."

Trey walked out and tried to hold his head up, but you could tell he was a broken man.

As he walked out of the office and through the building, Katrina's coworker came to ask her if everything was ok.

"Yes, everything is ok. I'm just going through a divorce like all of America. No need to concern yourself. Is there something you needed?"

"No ma'am, just checking on you and seeing if you were ok. Is there anything you need me to do while I'm here?"

"Not really. I just need you to get back to work and help any customer that comes in."

* * *

Friday came around, and Katrina and Trey were at the courthouse. Katrina had her lawyer with her, but Trey was alone. The look in his eyes showed how drained he was from this process. Trey contested nothing as he let Katrina have her way. She didn't want to split her home because she had it before they got married. She wanted everything that he had bought her because it would be considered a gift. She wanted to split their retirement in half even though he put more in it than she did. Finally, Katrina wanted alimony for spending time married to a cheater.

"Now Katrina, you are out of your fucking mind. I never cheated on you, and you should know that. Can you seriously sit here and show me proof that I cheated? I'm not agreeing to those terms. We can fight if that's what you really want."

"Naw, you right, I can't show proof right now, but I know.

As they argued back and forth, the judge demanded order in the court. "I'm sorry your honor, take the alimony off because I don't need to be reminded every month that I was married to this lying boy!"

Trey begged the judge to approve the terms so that it could be finalized and over with. In an unusual manner the judge reluctantly finalized the divorce along with the terms they agreed on. After court was finished, Trey waited on Katrina's lawyer for copies of the agreement. Katrina and Trey shared what they considered to be their last conversation.

"Now that our divorce is final and no one is in here, you can be honest. You probably thought you would never get caught. You know what they say, what's done in the dark will come to light."

"I never cheated. You were and will always be the woman I fell in love with. What the hell happened to you?!"

"You happened to me Trey, and the so-called man before you too. All men are the same!!!"

"Katrina, I don't know when it changed, but that day I left for school, I always regretted not choosing you over my career and dreams. This heartache I'm going through right now, I know it's God telling me to get away before I go crazy."

"I guess God told you to cheat too. Man, get out of my face with that shit." Katrina said and walked away.

CHAPTER SEVENTEEN
The Uh-Oh Moment

Trey shook his head and went to meet the lawyer. He grabbed his copy, walked down the hall, and got in the elevator. A few minutes later, Katrina came out of the courtroom and into the hallway. She looked down out the window and spotted trey talking on the phone as he walked to his car. He was walking with a sense of urgency. In her mind, she was thinking this dirty motherfucker couldn't wait until he got in his car and off the premises before getting on the phone talking to one of his hoes.

All of a sudden, the GIFT hit her hard. It knocked her into the nearest bench. As she struggled to get back to the window, her legs were shaking from climaxing. She was so confused, and as she got to the window to look for Trey, he was gone. Replaying everything that just happened and the gut feeling that gave her all she needed to know of his cheating, has now failed her.

How could this be possible? Dr. Oni told her this would only happen when he was having sex.

But how is this possible when she was just looking at him, and the GIFT was going on? The orgasm felt amazing, but the thought of it was bad. She called Trey to ask him to come back.

"Hello, why are you calling me?" Trey said before Katrina could get a word out. "Don't fucking call me anymore. You got what you wanted."

Trey hung up, but she continued to call him over and over. Katrina even used her lawyers' phone to call him.

Trey answered the phone. "Trey, could you come back real quick? We need to talk."

"Talk? About what, how you tried to break me? Please never call me again. I'm done!"

Katrina quickly called Tiffany to tell her what just happen.

"Tiff, I think I just made a huge mistake!!"

"What you mean, did you forget to ask for something in your divorce?" Tiffany asked her.

"Naw, he gave me everything but alimony. He said he never cheated."

"We both know he was lying; he was probably giving you some sob story like all men do."

"I think the GIFT lied to me."

"What? Why you say that?" Tiffany asked.

"I was just watching him out the window, and the GIFT hit me hard. I could clearly see he wasn't fucking, so how could this be?"

"Ok, now I'm confused. I thought the whole reason for having the GIFT was to know if he was cheating for sure. See, I told you that you were tripping. I told you it was just a sex spell, trans or whatever it was."

"But how can we explain Trey not picking up when I called? Or the times he went out with old girl and got caught up." Katrina said.

"What if he was not cheating and was actually telling the truth," Tiffany replied.

"Then I fucked up big time. We need to find Dr. Oni and get this shit off me. But what I'm most confused about is how the GIFT is triggered, like what makes it come on and off. It always comes on when I least expect it. What's going on with me! I'm a mess right now and don't know what to do. What if it was triggered by me thinking of him cheating all the time."

"How did he put the spell or whatever it was on you? Like what did he say or do?"

"He said something about my true love and how I would know every time he was having sex. How I would feel the effects of it."

"So, is Trey not your true love? You got another man or something you not telling me about?"

"Girl naw, and you know me and Trey were meant to be together."

"What about--?" Tiffany started to ask.

"Don't even mention his name. There is no way he could be my true love the way he did me. Plus, I haven't spoken to him in years and don't want to."

"But what if he was Katrina...? I mean he hurt you, but you were *all* about that man at one time."

"Well, I don't think it was him. I just need this off of me right now; that's all I know. Tiff, I need your help to track down Dr. Oni."

CHAPTER EIGHTEEN

Hunting Down Dr. Oni

Weeks went by, and neither one of them had gotten any closer to finding Dr. Oni. Tiffany and Katrina took a trip down to his old office in Louisiana. While there, they ran into the mailman standing by the mailboxes near Dr. Oni's old office. They asked the mailman questions, but he wouldn't help them because he was sworn to secrecy. As the mailman was placing the mail in their respective boxes, a letter fell on the floor with Dr. Oni's name on it. It seemed as if the mailman left the letter out on purpose to be of some service without getting into trouble. The letter had a forwarding address to Dr. Oni's place of residence somewhere in Africa. They both looked at each other in a clueless manner.

"How in the world are we supposed to find him now? Just go to Africa and ask everybody that doesn't speak English where can I find this man?" Katrina asked.

"I mean, we can try to look it up on google and try to find him now that we have an idea where he stays. Let's look on the map to see how big the village is and how much it will cost for you to go."

"For me to go. You not coming with me?"

"I don't know why you are acting like I don't have a job. I got bills to pay, and from the way it looks that ticket would cost too much right now."

"I'll pay for you, and you don't have to pay me back right now."

"Katrina, I have been there with you throughout this little issue, but I just told you I couldn't get off from my job like that. And also, *why* would I pay you back? I'm not the one that needs to go, nor do I have the desire to be over there. I'm fine right here. I can facetime you the whole time if you need me. I'll do *that* for you."

"So, you expect me to go to a foreign country by myself? What if something happens to me? I hope I get kidnapped and murdered. Imma put you down as my only living relative, and I hope they send the body to your front door heffa!

Shit, to be honest, I wouldn't be in this predicament if it weren't for you always asking me to go out with you and your problematic ass friends telling me of y'all problems. Got me all paranoid in my marriage." Katrina vented at Tiffany.

"Don't you mean *used* to be marriage!?

"You ain't shit for that comment heffa."

"Ok, ok, ok, ok, I'll go, but I can't pay you back. I ain't got it like that," Tiffany replied.

"Deal! So, we need to leave this week or early next week."

"Dang Katrina, what am I supposed to tell my boss?"

"Tell him you had a wreck and need a few days off."

"You know damn well black people don't like going to the doctor as is. You want me to get a doctor's bill for no reason? Girl, you are crazy. I can't afford to do that. I'll figure something out. Just let me know when, and you better not ask me to pay you back. I'm serious!"

CHAPTER NINETEEN
Explain, Katrina.

The next day Katrina tried calling Trey to see if he would talk to her. Trey had no intentions of talking to her. Trey told Katrina he thought that it was best if they lost each other's number and not try to contact each other anymore. Yet, Katrina was very adamant about talking to him. Trey finally agreed to talk to her one day during the week, which would delay her trip to Africa because she didn't know which day it would be. Katrina was so nervous to tell him what happened and ask for his forgiveness. So many things went through her mind as she tried to play out scenes of how things would go. All scenarios ended up with her alone and feeling foolish.

The days passed by so fast, and Katrina's anxiety never settled down. The week was almost over, and she still had yet to hear from Trey. She tried calling him, but his phone went straight to voicemail multiple times. The only thing to do was to pop up at his job because she didn't know where he lived.

She pulled up to his office and saw his car in the parking lot. She called the office, and the secretary answered the phone. She asked if Trey was there, and the secretary replied yes, but that he was busy right now and could take a message. Katrina said no and sat in her car. She decided to park in another parking lot and wait on Trey to come out.

Hours went by, and Katrina was getting impatient, so she called his office again. This time the secretary told Katrina that he stepped out for lunch about an hour ago and that she should call back around 3:30 or 4 o'clock. Katrina looked at her watch. It was now 2:18 pm, and she had been sitting there since noon. What game are you playing, as she yelled at the secretary? The phone hung up, and this pissed her off badly. The only thing on her mind was to kick in the door and cause the biggest scene ever. As she pulled into the office's parking lot, a black BMW with very dark tinted windows pulled up. Trey got out on the passenger side. He started yelling at Katrina for being there. Trey was really getting out of character with some of the things he yelled at her.

"Katrina, why the hell are you here? You are at my place of business looking like you are ready to start some shit. If that's the case, get your ass off my lot before I call the police!"

"Yeah, I'm pissed! You got your secretary lying for you and shit. This is some bull, and you know it, who is in the car? Is it another woman already? I knew I shouldn't have come. Why did you lie to me about making time to talk if you didn't want to talk?"

"Well, first off, that's my best friend Deon. He just made it back in town from doing business. Second, I owe you *no* explanation because we are done and no longer have anything to talk about."

"Trey, I messed up, and I'm sorry. Please just listen to me for 5 minutes, I beg you," Katrina pleaded.

"Go ahead; it's always about you and what you want. Make it quick. I have other things to tend to."

"What other things?"

"See, that's your problem. You don't control me, and you *don't* need to know everything. Are you about to spend the last 5 minutes that I'm giving you to talk about what I'm doing because you just must know?"

"I'm sorry. Is that how you always felt about me? Trey, I came here to tell you something, but clearly you have something to say."

"As a matter of fact, I do. I believe this all started because I wouldn't let you control me."

"No, it's not!"

"B.S. I can remember the first time it happened you were so upset."

"When what happened?"

"I remember when I went off to college, I chose my dream job over my dream girl, and you broke up with me because things didn't go your way. Even though I tried to keep us together, it was so easy for you to call it quits. It's always been about you. Even when you moved back, and you found a house you liked. It just so happened I was around and the primary realtor for that particular home. You made me talk to those folks to lower the price for you, and I made *nothing* from that sale. Not *once* did you think of the fact that that's how I made my living until I passed the bar exam."

"But I let you stay with me to save money though," Katrina replied.

"That's not the point I'm making. You made your mind up about everything and had to have it your way. I think you let me stay with you because that house was a tad bit out of your budget, and my extra income was a supplement for you. It's like when you want something, you have to have it. You were and are bad with money. That's also why I think you wanted me to pay you alimony."

"No, that's not true at all. I just wanted payback from you cheating on me."

"I never cheated on you; stop saying that. You have accused me enough, and I'm tired of it. I just thought you were being insecure, but when you started popping up on me all the time, I figured something wasn't right. Why do you think I cheated?"

"Well, it started one night when your phone rang around midnight, and you chose not to answer it. My friends have all had that happen to them, and they knew right then that their men were cheating. You did what all men do."

"What was that?" Trey asked.

"You tried to act like there was nothing to it and never answered it when it rang."

"You think just by telling me to chill out and let it go, that put my mind at ease? Then you weren't answering my calls all the times I called."

"See Katrina, it's all about you, and needing to always be in control. And in the end, it caused you to *lose* control. That was Deon calling me from overseas."

"Why would Deon be calling you from overseas? Don't he stay somewhere around here?"

"Yes, but since you must know again. Deon was calling about business. We constructed a deal to sell industrial steel to overseas companies as a side hustle. I had to get a second income because you were constantly spending money, but I never complained. I just didn't want to tell you and argue about it, but I was tired of feeling like you were in control. My thing was, since we stayed at your house, you felt as if you were the commander and chief. The day you told me you wanted a divorce; I was willing to submit and tell you what was going on. That it was just bad communication on my behalf, but you were so damn stubborn you wouldn't listen," Trey explained.

"That sounds a little farfetched, but I have no room to talk. So why was he calling you from a google number?"

"I just realized you never been out of the country." Trey chuckled.

"What's funny about that Trey?" Katrina asked.

"Well overseas, they don't have the same cellular towers we have, so his phone wouldn't work over there. Therefore, he had to call me from a google number when he's around Wi-Fi or some type of internet."

"What about the *times* of day and night that he called you at?

"That depended on the country he was in. Some countries are in totally different time zones. Places like China could be 12 hours ahead or behind us in the US. So when he called, 11 am would be 11 pm for us. Katrina looked over at Deon, who seemed to have been listening the whole time. Deon had this look on his face as if she should have listened to Trey before all this happened. I told him not to call me so late because I was trying to keep this under wraps, but you know Deon. His hard-headed ass did what he wanted. Those would be the times he left me voicemails so that I would have some type of idea of what was going on with the plans and contracts.

"Trey, that seems so small to hide from me though. I didn't know that you felt like that about me."

"This is something I could have told you if you would have agreed to go to marriage counseling," Trey explained.

"Well, I have a confession to make. Don't be mad at me because I was trying to catch you cheating. I went so far as to hire a private eye or two. I wasn't satisfied with the first one's work, but the last guy I hired happened to be a witch doctor."

"What the hell were you trying to do to me?" he asked.

"I was desperate to find out something. I swear he didn't put a spell on you. He only placed one on me, and it drove me insane. It was a way for me to find out if you were cheating or not. The spell would let me know if you were intimate with anyone."

"Now this just seems so stupid. I'm supposed to believe you let witchdoctor put a spell on you, and it was supposed to tell you if I cheated or not, or more like get laid. Well, it told you wrong, and you went through all this trouble for nothing. It sounds like you need to go get your money back because it just caused you a divorce! So, do you get this feeling all the time? What is the feeling?"

"It's hard to explain, especially now with me being confused on how it comes about."

"Well, try to explain, I'm listening. I just wanna know why I had to go through this when you should have known better. I could never cheat on you. What did he say or do to you with this spell?"

"Well, it was a spell over the phone."

"Over the phone?!"

"Yeah, it was something he said to me over the phone, and that was all he did. We hung up, and I been getting a feeling ever since."

"Do you remember the spell, like what were his exact words?"

Katrina was very hesitant to tell Trey because she knew that she hurt him already and didn't know how he would react to this.

"I don't know exactly what he said, but it was something about knowing when your lover is sharing intimacy with someone else."

"Katrina, I seriously don't believe that's all he said. See, you are still lying and holding things back from me. You still haven't changed, so why did you even come down here?"

"That is the truth. I'm serious! That's all he said. Ever since then, I have been getting that feeling and have yet to figure out what's going on with me."

"Katrina, I mean no harm when I say this, but you need help. Just maybe you have snapped from always wanting to be in control, and now you are not even in control of yourself right now. I have a friend that might be able to help you, but you gotta take things seriously."

"Trey, I'm fine. I don't need to see anybody. I got it covered, and things will get better real soon. Can we just start over and work on us?" Katrina asked him.

"Let me sleep on it, and I will get back to you soon." Trey replied.

CHAPTER TWENTY
Africa, Here We Come

Days went by, and Katrina heard nothing back from Trey. She thought he had given up. The phone rang, and she got so excited to answer it but forgot to look at the caller ID.

"I've been waiting on your call! Why did it take you so long? Katrina said into the phone.

"Naw, I have been waiting on *your* call to see when we're leaving," Tiffany replied.

"Things have been pushed back for a couple of weeks. I just gotta buy the tickets now and get a passport, so I'm told."

"What you mean, so you're told. You don't have a passport?"

"No, I do not have a passport! Trey made fun of me the other day because he realized that I had never left the country before. Why do *you* have a passport? I thought you didn't want to go to Africa."

"I don't want to go to Africa, but I have been to Germany and other places that require you have one, duh. So, when do you think you will have it?" Tiffany asked.

"I am on my way to the post office right now. I heard if I put on a rush on it, I should have it in two weeks. As soon as I get it, I will book our tickets, and we'll be on the first plane out of here!"

* * *

Weeks passed, and Katrina now had her passport but had yet to hear from Trey, but she understood. In her mind, when she got back, she was going to fight hard to get her man back. She finally booked the trip for her and Tiffany to go to Africa, and they left on the fastest flight out of there to find Dr. Oni.

"Girl, this trip is so crazy. I don't see why anyone would want to be on a plane that long. All that turbulence and layovers was driving me crazy!" Katrina looked at Tiffany and told her.

"I didn't mind the flight. I sat next to a person who didn't believe in deodorant. That man stunk so bad I was about to die!"

Katrina laughed. "I didn't have that problem, but my neck hurt from trying to sleep with my head nodding back and forth."

"Well, let's get to a hotel, relax and then try to find this man for you. Did you book the hotel?"

"I forgot, but imma do that right now. Damn, I'm not getting a signal. What in the world is going on?"

"Ain't no American cell towers here?"

Katrina laughed to herself, thinking of how Trey made fun of her, and now she knew why.

"We need to find Wi-Fi and a place to eat. I'm so hungry right now it doesn't make sense. Do they have a Starbucks or even a Wendy's around here?" Katrina said.

"I don't know. This is my first time in Africa!" Tiffany responded sarcastically.

They went through the airport asking people about places to eat and where they could access the internet. Luckily, there were a lot of English-speaking tourists that came through looking for the same thing. They met a group of people from the US that seemed pretty cool and tagged along with them. Once they got to a local hotspot in the city with free Wi-Fi, it seemed as if luck was finally back on their side. Katrina booked the room immediately, finding a 4-star hotel nearby with all the amenities.

When they got to the hotel, they tried looking up Dr. Oni.

"Where is the letter with his address on it?" Tiffany asked.

With this dumb look on her face, Katrina replied "THE LETTER!!!!!!"

"Do not play with me right now. Please tell me you are playing..."

"I'm not playing. I forgot it back home, and I know exactly where it is. It's on my kitchen counter. I'll just call my mom and have her give us the address."

Katrina's mother didn't answer the phone, so she called her father. He answered but was unable to talk right then because he was working. So, it seemed as though no one was able to help.

"Call Trey; he will help for sure. Have him go to your parents' house to get the key to your place." Tiffany told Katrina.

"Trey doesn't want to talk to me, let alone go back to my house to help me out. He hasn't talked to me much after the divorce. He has been ignoring me, and I believe he has moved on. I don't want to keep blowing him up just to find out that he could care less about what I need."

"You never know, just try to call him."

Tiffany decided to give him a call.

CHAPTER TWENTY-ONE
The Interaction

The phone rang a bunch of times but no answer. So, she called again, but this time he answered.

"Hello!!!" Trey answered with anger in his voice.

"Trey, it's me."

"Katrina? I kind of figured it would be you. Why are you calling me from this weird number?"

"I'm out of the country, and this was the only way I could contact you. Why are you so mad right now?"

"You really want to ask me that? I told you to let me think about us trying to talk again, and now you are pressuring me."

"Really Trey, you are tripping. I called you because I need a favor, not trying to beg you back. I'm giving you your space to figure it out."

"I can't tell! So, what did you call me for? What favor do you need from me?"

"I need you to go to my house and get something for me. There is a letter with Dr. Oni's name and his forwarding address on the kitchen counter. I need that like really bad."

"What makes you think I have a key to your house? Because I don't."

"I think you still might have the key I put in your car for emergencies."

"I'm pretty sure I gave you all your keys back, and I never saw a key in my car."

"Check the owner's manual to your car. I put a spare key in both of our cars like that."

Trey put Katrina on hold to check and found the key in the exact spot she said it would be.

"Yeah, I found the key, but why would you hide it from me and not let me know about it?"

"It wasn't for you; it was for me. You know how forgetful I could be at times. I even forgot I put it in your car. That just goes to show you my mind ain't right at times. Can you please do this for me Trey?"

"Is it that important you need me to go instead of your parents or somebody else?"

"I wouldn't have bothered to call you if I had somebody else that could do it, but I don't, and it was Tiffany's idea anyway."

"Tiffany? So y'all just traveling the world since you single now. So have Tiffany's family do it. I 've got work to do."

"Trey, it's not like that at all, I promise. Just do this one favor for me, and I won't call you again until you decide to talk to me when you're ready."

"Ok, I'll do it when I get done with what I have to do. Check your email in a few hours. I'll let you know when I have it."

* * *

In Katrina's mind, Trey was giving her the run around again. After a few hours, there was no email from Trey. She was getting very impatient with Trey and his dishonest antics. She called his phone but got no answer. She called him numerous times to see what the heck was going on and to find out why he continued to lie to her. She was so desperate that she called her home phone and Trey picked up.

"Trey, what the hell is going on? I have been calling you for a while now. You won't pick up your phone, but you pick up mine? What's that about?"

"Katrina, I ain't got time to argue with you about my phone. I'm at your house now and trying to do what you asked me to do. I answered your phone to tell your man or whoever was calling that you can't talk right now and to call back later."

"That's really petty of you to assume I have a man knowing I'm trying to get back with you. Anyway, do you see the letter on the counter?"

"I see a few letters. What am I looking for exactly?"

"There is a letter with Dr. Oni's name and address on it. Just tell me the address, and I'll let you get back to snooping."

Trey gave her the information, and they got off the phone. Katrina looked at Tiffany and shook her head. Now they were looking at the directions to Dr. Oni's current address. They found the shortest route and a taxi to take them.

On their way to see him, Katrina got an anxiety attack, and Tiffany did everything she could to calm her down. The cab pulled up to the building and dropped them off at his new office. After calming down, Katrina and Tiffany looked around to see the numbers on the doors. They found the right door addressed to Dr. Oni.

Tiffany looked through the window and saw a man sitting at a desk. She quickly got Katrina's attention and asked her if she knew what he looked like. Katrina didn't recall him having a profile picture on his site. They both looked through the window to get a good look at him. The man looked over at them and waved.

"Is that the man?" Tiffany asked Katrina.

"I don't think so. The man I saw on the website was an average-looking man with a clean cut," Katrina replied.

"Let's go in and ask him about Dr. Oni."

They went in and were quickly approached by the man. He asked them if they had an appointment. Stating that he was not seeing walk-ins today, but if they *did* have an appointment to take a seat.

"No sir, I do not have an appointment and just need a little information if you don't mind. I swear it will be quick. I just need to know if you know of a Dr. Oni and where can I find him?"

The man looked strangely at them and asked why they needed to see him. Katrina told him a short story of dealing with him without giving her name to him. The man blurted her name out without hesitation.

"Katrina! I remember talking to you. Did you get your answer? Before you answer that, how did you find me? Dr. Oni said as he revealed himself.

"I went to your old office in Louisiana, and there was a letter on the floor with this forwarding address. Wait a minute, you don't look like the guy on your site. What's that about? Why are you making fake IDs?"

"Fake ID's? That's not true. I used a colleague's picture to make clients feel a little easy about working with me. People are shallow in the U.S. So, what is it you need me to do?"

"I need you to remove this curse from me. I don't understand it, and I don't want it anymore," Katrina told him.

"I can't remove it," Dr. Oni replied.

"More like you won't remove it, and why? She paid you!" Tiffany yelled.

"For one, she did not pay me, and for two, it's women like y'all who don't understand when you got it good—always needing just a *little* something more. You don't know what it is, but it is just eating away at you to have it all. Tell me Katrina, did you read my bio and back story on my page? Or did you just see my practice and success rate? See, you never took the time to look at those things. The lesson in it all is to realize what you have in front of you," Dr. Oni said.

"Sounds like a personal problem to me," Tiffany replied

"Yes, it is! My ex-wife had it made with me, but my looks became a problem after she spent enough of my money. Then she told me she wasn't in love with me. I constantly played my divorce over and over in my head, trying to figure out what I was missing. See, I was in love with her, but she was never in love with me. Therefore, she could never truly see how good things were. Now she is back with her ex that did her wrong in so many ways. But she is happy because that's who she was still in love with before meeting me. These are things one needs to understand for themselves and stop wasting other peoples time.

"What do you mean wasting people's time? I didn't waste my husband's time! How can you fix your mouth to say that to me, and you don't even know me?"

"How was your relationship before you found me? I bet you had it made. Tell me, what made you question your husband's loyalty to you?" Dr. Oni asked.

"I was out with Tiffany and few friends. They started telling me the signs of cheating and how their husbands were not slick enough. I then started noticing some things in my own marriage."

"Don't blame me for this! You are a grown woman," Tiffany jumped in.

"If I would have stayed my butt at home instead of going out with you, things would probably still be good," Katrina told Tiffany.

"You're right, probably because you are so perfect."

"Ladies let's not do this in my office. Now, if you can excuse yourselves from here, I have other appointments and clients to tend to soon.

"Hell no, I'm not leaving until you take this spell off of me. It ruined my life!" Katrina yelled to Dr. Oni.

"I don't have to do *anything* for you. I promised you results, and you got them. As a matter of fact, you owe me money for getting you results!"

"What results? All I did was have sporadic orgasms. I don't understand how, but that's all it was."

"Doc, take it from her and give it to me," Tiffany said

"No, no, no, it doesn't work like that. Do you remember what I told you when I did it?" Dr. Oni asked

"You said something about me feeling the pleasure of my true love cheating on me."

"If that be the case, then your husband was not your true love. I told you my policy before we went through with it. Either you pay me, or you can leave my office right now, please," Dr. Oni told Katrina.

CHAPTER TWENTY-TWO

Self-Reflection

Katrina and Tiffany left the office talking about what just happened in Dr. Oni's office. Katrina was in disbelief with how he talked to her, and Tiffany was still in her feelings a little bit. She felt as if Katrina blamed her and had yet to apologize for what she said. They made it back to the hotel and went to Katrina's room. Katrina plopped down on the bed, buried her face into the pillows, and let out a frustrating scream. Tiffany asked Katrina to get up for a minute so they could talk a little more about the situation.

"So, what are you going to do when you get back home?" Tiffany asked her.

"I don't know. I just want this to all end. This is like a bad dream, and we are stuck in it.

"Let's get one thing straight and off my chest. I didn't cause any trouble in your marriage. You did that all by yourself!" Tiffany told her.

"Since we're being real with each other, yes, I blame you. You always have a way to make me do something I refuse to do at first, but then I give in to you. Going out drinking and partying with the homies was *your* idea!"

"So you mean to tell me that you can't just go out and not be influenced? You chose to listen to them and bring that home. We went out, and that's how you should have left it!"

"Wow, you really wanna go there with me? Same ole Tiffany, just like in college when you almost got me raped! You talked me into going to the party that night, and you left me hanging to go ho around.

"I got you to go to the party, but I did *not* make you drink like that. Once again, not taking responsibility led you into that position. I'm the one who ran and got Dallas to help your ass." Tiffany said back in frustration.

"See, that's another good point. You even introduced me to that asshole and look what happened. Now that I think of it, yes, I blame you for a lot. You are always around when things start to go bad."

"Start to go bad?" Tiffany questioned.

"Yes, all the bad things started with you talking me into everything. It's like your ass could never understand when I said no."

"It's like *your* ass couldn't stand firm on your no. I didn't put a gun to your head and make you do anything." Tiffany replied.

"You might as well have for the pain you caused me."

Tiffany stormed out of the room. Katrina laid back down as tears started to flow down her cheeks. She was thinking about what she just went through and how she doesn't have anyone to call on. She texted Tiffany to apologize, but Tiffany didn't reply back to her. Katrina got up and walked to Tiffany's room. She knocked on the door, but no one answered. She walked to the lobby and asked the clerk if she had seen someone that fit the description she gave. The clerk answered back, saying yes and that they just called a cab for the individual.

Time went by, and still no reply back from Tiffany. It was getting late, and Katrina was getting worried about her friend. She walked back to Tiffany's room. This time she beat on the door so loudly that a nearby neighbor stuck their head to see what was going on. Tiffany opened the door in a rude manner, asking Katrina what she wanted.

"Tiffany, where have you been?" Katrina yelled.

"I'm grown, and I don't have to tell you shit!"

"Look, I know you're mad, and we both said some things that we might've regretted, but you're still my girl, and I was worried. You could have let me know where you were going so at least I would know where to come looking for you if need be."

"Naw, I didn't because you would have thought I was making you come with me. What do you want?" Tiffany asked.

Katrina looked at her and said, "I came to apologize, but you are being really bitchy right now."

"How would you feel if I blamed you for all the bad stuff happened in my life? That ain't fair nor cool with me, and so far, you haven't apologized," Tiffany replied.

"Well, you're right, and I'm so sorry. We have been friends for too long, and I was wrong to blame you. Please forgive me."

"I already did! I just wanted your stubborn ass to admit you were wrong. I'm sorry too, but I don't know for what, though," Tiffany replied as they both laughed.

"I got a serious question, though. What if the doctor's spell was for your *true* love? Dallas really could've been your true love if you think about it."

"I was thinking that too. But Dallas could never have another chance with me, so why would I still be in love with him?"

"Do you still hate him?"

"Yes, with every fiber in my body. I can't even stand to hear his name!"

"Well, you are still hurting and not over what he did. He had *that* much influence on your heart. That's because you were so in love with him."

"I was getting over him when I got back with Trey."

"But did you *get over* him, or were you trying to *forget about* him?"

They finished up having their conversation and discussed what time they were leaving in the morning.

* * *

They got back to the states, and Katrina was now on a mission to heal. Along with that, she planned to fight for Trey's love again.

CHAPTER TWENTY-THREE
The Failed Plan

Katrina attempted to call Trey but got no answer. She went to Trey's parents' house to see if he was over there. She didn't know where he lived, and going to his job again was a no-no. She pulled up in the yard and saw his father outside cutting grass. She got out and greeted his father with a formal hello. He was looking at her like, why was she there. He asked her what was going on and immediately told her Trey was not there.

Katrina stated that she realized that, but was just wondering if he could let her know where Trey lived. He stated that it was not his place to give Trey's address out. Katrina looked towards the front door of the house and saw Trey's mother looking out of the screen door. Katrina walked to the door and asked his mother to let Trey know that she came by and that it was important that he called her. Out of curiosity, his mother came out and asked Katrina what was so important that she couldn't just tell them about it. They would judge if it was important or not.

Katrina didn't go into full detail, but she told them that she really messed up her marriage and was willing to do anything to get Trey back. Katrina's body language seemed true enough to his parents. They called Trey and told him to come over because his father needed help getting something in the house.

An hour went by, and Trey finally pulled up. Seeing Katrina there confused him. Trey got out of the car and asked his parents what was going on. What is it that pops needed help with as he ignored the fact that Katrina was staring right at his face. His parents apologized and said to just give her a chance to explain. Although he felt betrayed, Trey still gave her a chance to talk. His parents went into the house and gave them their privacy.

Katrina started, "Trey, I didn't know what else to do. I know I did you wrong, and you didn't deserve that. You were right. I am selfish and a total cunt. I'm not trying to make this about me. It's about us."

"If you want me to give you a chance, I need the whole truth. Tell me about this curse you put on me. Did you really hire a witch doctor, and why did you go to Africa?"

"I did not have a curse placed on you, I promise. I went to Africa to find the witch doctor. Ever since I did that stupid thing, things have been going all wrong for me. I lost the best man in my life because I had to have control. I'm sorry, and I love you, Trey," Katrina replied.

"Katrina, what did he tell you? What was the spell?

"Trey, it's so confusing. I'm lost just thinking about it."

"So you want me to listen to you, but yet you still don't want to tell me the truth about it. Even though I think this is crazy, I still want to know it all just like you wanted to know all my details."

"Ok Trey, here it is. The doctor's spell was about revealing my faults. I was so caught up on catching you cheating that he put a spell on me that I couldn't even *begin* to imagine."

"What did he say or do, and I'm *not* asking you again," Trey warned.

"The spell was that I would get the sexual pleasures from the woman or women my true love was having sex with at that time. Then I would know when you were cheating. The crazy thing is, every time the feeling came about, I couldn't get in touch with you at that moment. Crazy, huh?"

"Yeah, I must admit that does sound a little crazy. So who was your true love, Dallas?"

"Come on Trey. You know darn well me and that dude are done for. The way he did me, how could he be my true love? I always thought it was you, silly."

"Is that the truth? Is that all you wanted to say to me?"

"I went crazy with this idea of you cheating on me that I must have imagined you in my heart having an affair. It really did a number on me."

"Did you have sex with that dude I saw you in the park with?" Trey asked.

"No, I didn't."

"Did you want to? Did he have a chance to? Do you want to be with him?"

"Trey, honestly no, and that is the truth. Baby, I want you back! Are you dating anybody? Did you link back up with your old colleague?"

"Naw, I never called her again after the incident between us. You have some making up to do if I *ever* give you another chance."

"Baby, I promise to make it up to you. Do you want me to run your bathwater?" Katrina replied jokingly.

"Hell no, every time you did that, it came with something attached to it!"

They both started laughing as Trey hugged Katrina. The hug lasted a while as they were finally reunited.

* * *

They dated for the next couple of days with a whole plan on ways to make their relationship stronger, and things were going great. Trey hadn't moved back in but was staying at Katrina's house an awful lot lately. One morning Trey got up to get ready for work. He went through his normal routine as Katrina tried to sleep but couldn't because Trey was making so much noise. Trey walked downstairs to get ready to leave for work.

Katrina was suddenly hit with an extreme amount of pleasure. She looked around and was confused about why this was happening again. But this time it was *so* good! She laid back as she opened her legs and bit her lip. She squirmed all over the bed as her legs shook.

She grabbed her pillow and moaned. When she was done, she was breathing so hard. She got up and headed to the bathroom to clean herself off.

Trey was standing in the doorway with a grimacing look on his face as their eyes met. Not being able to explain quickly enough, Katrina froze as Trey walked back down the stairs. Katrina gathered herself and chased after him.

"Trey, why were you staring at me like that? I thought you left for work!"

"I was going to work, but when I opened the door, I turned around because I wanted to kiss you and maybe get some before I left. I see I was late to the party."

"I don't know what to say. It's been a minute since I got the feeling. Baby come back upstairs. I got you."

"You got me? Naw, *it* got you, and I'm running late."

Katrina was thrown back by this as she watched Trey get in his car and leave. This was the last thing she wanted to happen because she didn't want to lose Trey to this. She sat down on the couch and put her head down in her hands and started to cry. Eventually, it was time for her to get ready for work.

She got to the office and took a minute for herself. She sat back in the chair and went over what just happened at the house. A coworker came by and broke her train of thought, letting her know that the bank president would be in today. This was an important day, and she could not let her personal affairs cloud her mind. So she got her thoughts together and went to her regular morning meeting.

Things went well, and after the meeting, she made it back to her office. Trey called to ask her about dinner for that night, and he mentioned that he saw her that morning. He told her that she could have waited on him. That if she was horny and wanted him, she could have just said something instead of pleasing herself. Trey told her next time to wait on him, but it did turn him on *big* time.

She asked him why he didn't join in (Knowing that it was the GIFT and not him that had her in a frenzy). He seemed to be in a good mood, and this gave Katrina a boost of positive energy. She felt like she didn't have to talk about it again and could move on.

Word reached her that the bank president was in the building and was going to every office one by one.

Katrina told Trey that she had to get off the phone and that she loved him. She prepared her office for the president to come in and be comfortable. Ready to answer any question for him, she heard a knock on her door. It was her branch manager and the bank president. She stood up and greeted him with a firm handshake as he acknowledged her. He shared that he had heard a lot about the work she had done there. Impressed by the compliments given by her peers and to see she is so young was a shock. He stated that she looked familiar.

What college did you attend? Katrina told him, and before she could say anything else, he blurted out the sorority she was in. He smiled and told her that he graduated from the same college and that her sorority was the sister chapter to his fraternity. Not meaning to show any disrespect, but she stated the obvious. He was much older than her, and that she didn't remember seeing him on campus.

There was no harm taken. Although he wasn't there, he was very present at that school's fraternity trying to guide and mentor young men. One of those young men he mentored was Dallas. There was a function happening on campus that the fraternity was sponsoring.

She and Dallas were very vocal and impactful at this event. He hoped he hadn't crossed the line by bringing up old memories. That day stuck out for him because they were such a confident and powerful couple. He compared them to a young Michelle and Barack Obama. She told him she remembered the function, but it was such a long time ago, and that she hopes he doesn't hold it against her for not remembering everyone out there. There were so many people at that function, and people were having so much fun.

She told him that she was married now, and things are going great with the decision she made to come back home to this job and her high school sweetheart. The president of the bank was happy she was working for him as well. Again, he told her he meant no harm. He just didn't see her wearing a ring and was just making small talk. He explained how she stuck out then like she stuck out now working for him. They finished their meet and greet and he left her office.

The evening came, and she was now off of work. Katrina was ready to wind down and get home to see what Trey wanted to eat. She called Trey but got no answer. Things started running through her mind about that morning all over again.

She hoped that Trey would not hold it against her. Katrina would understand if he was having a hard time dealing with that. As she pulled up to the house, she saw that her lights were on in the house. She could hear soft sexy music playing inside of the house. As she stuck the keys in the door, the light went off, which alarmed her a little. She saw that Trey's car was in the yard but didn't understand what was going on.

She took a step back to gather herself. She was hoping that there was no other woman in the house, and this was Trey's way of getting her back. As she opened the door, Trey stood there with a robe on and wine in both hands.

"Come on in babe, I have your bath water ready, and I am going to cater to you tonight. As I recall, you were the last one to do this, but tonight, it's mine."

"Trey, I don't know what's going on, but I'm feeling it right now. Wait a minute, what's going on? Baby, let me explain."

Trey puts his finger over her lips.

"Take this wine and get your fine ass in that water upstairs before it gets cold. We can talk up there."

As they walked upstairs, Katrina felt confused but went along with his plan. She got in the water and relaxed. She had been in there for at least ten minutes, and Trey had yet to come in there. She got out of the water and went to see what was going on. When she opened the door, Trey was lying in bed with the cover over half of his body."

Trey said, "Baby, when I came back upstairs this morning, I saw you tossing and turning in bed from wanting me so bad. I watched you, and it turned me on. Why didn't you just tell me you wanted it. I would have given it to you. But right now, at this moment, get your ass in this bed!"

This turned Katrina on in ways that she has never been turned on before. Trey started kissing her and moving his hands all over her body. He leaned back and told her to move like she moved that morning.

"Katrina, I want you to do what you were doing without me but on me. Baby, get wild!"

"I am Trey. Talk dirty to me."

Trey continued to move on her in ways that he hadn't done before. But he started to feel like she didn't want him like she did this morning. Trey stopped and stood up.

"What are you doing?" Katrina asked him.

"I want to watch you please yourself first. What image of me were you thinking this morning?" Trey asked as he stood there naked.

Katrina was so confused, but now she understood what was going on. Trey *didn't* know it was the GIFT that did it, that gave her that thrill. So, Katrina had to act fast and try to imitate the movements from that morning, but she didn't remember them. Trey started to question if she even wanted him like this morning or was it someone else. Katrina sat up in bed and attempted to tell Trey the truth because she knew he realized something wasn't the same. She tried to start an argument, but Trey was not bothered by it, and what he had to say next would shock her.

"Trey," Katrina said, "I don't know what you want from me. I was turned on. But now you are asking me to do all this freaky stuff in front of you, and it makes me uncomfortable. What's the deal?"

"As I am watching you now, the display you put on this morning was not for me. What's going on?"

Although Katrina felt like it was the wrong time to tell him, she felt he needed to hear the truth again.

"Baby, if I tell you, you can't get mad."

"Are you trying to tell me it's the curse Dr. Oni put on you?"

"Yes, it is, but I didn't try to have it Trey, I swear."

"Does it make you go that crazy?"

"I didn't realize I was going that crazy. Why were you just standing there watching me instead of saying something?"

"I thought I just caught you playing with yourself because of me, but now I know ain't nothing for *me* anymore. Is this feeling coming from something or somebody? Like what did he say again, something about your true love?"

"Trey, I'm trying, and I promise I love you."

"But you're not *in* love with me!"

"Honestly, I *think* I am Trey!"

"What do you mean you think? You should know like I do. I know this may seem dumb, but I knew it deep down inside."

Trey put his clothes back on and kissed Katrina goodbye as she teared up but didn't attempt to stop him. As Trey left, he turned back and said something to her...

* * *

Katrina ends her story there with the older lady as she heard over the loudspeakers that her flight is now boarding. The only advice the woman could give her after listening was that was GOD wanted her to go through that.

Katrina looked at the woman weird for saying that. The woman explains that if she hadn't exercised her free will to believe more in black magic than her faith, she would not have been in this situation. That if she strives to put God first in whatever she does, then the next man or the man she wants will be right for her, and she will know it. Maybe Trey is still waiting on you. God has a way of changing hearts if it's meant to be. Just believe in him instead of worldly things. Now it's time to board the plane and get your life back.

www.ingramcontent.com/pod-product-compliance
Lightning Source LLC
Chambersburg PA
CBHW050410030726
47503CB00006B/2118